GW00375327

'Hard-worn Sydney PI Cliff H
mean streets all the way back i
Hardy has been shot at many t
licence and regained it, solved lo
head more times than you can co
Corris come close to writing a bad Hardy novel ...

'As usual, the pacing is brisk and Corris smoothly mixes genuine
thrills with sharp-eyed descriptions of Sydney and astute political
observations.'   *Canberra Times*

'This is classic Corris, a joy to read as he takes his readers to the
heart of a good crime mystery.'   *Newcastle Herald*

'You can settle into a Cliff Hardy novel as into a favourite
armchair. You are quite likely not to get up until the book comes
to an end, page-turningly beguiled by the lucid, easy prose, the
laconic humour, the ingenious plot—often, as in this case, situated
somewhere in the grey area between the legally and the morally
legitimate—and the character of Hardy himself ...'

Adelaide Advertiser

'It's hard not to agree with writer Shane Maloney when he says
what Ian Rankin does for Edinbugh, Peter Corris does for Sydney.'
South Coast Register

'Through the unwavering gaze of Cliff Hardy, Corris has
conducted a longitudinal investigation of Australian society over
the past 35 years, providing a searing and wry commentary on social
injustice, corruption, and urban development. Like Hammett and
Chandler, the godfathers of American crime fiction who were his
early influences, along with John D. MacDonald, Corris portrays
society itself as the crime.'   *Sydney Morning Herald*

'*Gun Control* ... is a cracker of a novel ... Corris has always enjoyed
weaving his serial narratives in and out of the politics of the day.
Like his hero, he seldom points fingers, but reveals a sadness at the
way things are.'   *Weekend Australian*

PETER CORRIS is known as the 'godfather' of Australian crime fiction through his Cliff Hardy detective stories. He has written in many other areas, including a co-authored autobiography of the late Professor Fred Hollows, a history of boxing in Australia, spy novels, historical novels and a collection of short stories about golf (see www.petercorris. net). In 1999, Peter Corris was awarded the Lifetime Achievement Award from the Crime Writers Association of Australia and in 2009, the Ned Kelly Award for Best Fiction for *Deep Water*. He is married to writer Jean Bedford and has lived in Sydney for most of his life. They have three daughters and six grandsons.

Peter Corris's Cliff Hardy novels include *The Empty Beach*, *Master's Mates*, *The Coast Road*, *Saving Billie*, *The Undertow*, *Appeal Denied*, *The Big Score*, *Open File*, *Deep Water*, *Torn Apart*, *Follow the Money*, *Comeback*, *The Dunbar Case* and *Silent Kill*. *Gun Control* is his fortieth Cliff Hardy book.

He writes a regular weekly column for the online journal *Newtown Review of Books* (www.newtownreviewofbooks. com.au).

PETER CORRIS

GUN CONTROL

ALLEN&UNWIN

SYDNEY•MELBOURNE•AUCKLAND•LONDON

Thanks to Jean Bedford
and to many at Allen & Unwin

This edition first published in 2015
First published in 2015

Copyright © Peter Corris 2015

Allen & Unwin
83 Alexander Street
Crows Nest NSW 2065
Australia
Phone:(61 2) 8425 0100
Email: info@allenandunwin.com
Web: www.allenandunwin.com

Cataloguing-in-Publication details are available
from the National Library of Australia
www.trove.nla.gov.au

ISBN 978 1 76029 106 8

Internal design by Emily O'Neill
Set in Adobe Caslon by Midland Typesetters, Australia
Printed and bound in Australia by Griffin Press

10 9 8 7 6 5 4 3 2

MIX
Paper from
responsible sources
FSC www.fsc.org   FSC® C009448

The paper in this book is FSC® certified.
FSC® promotes environmentally responsible,
socially beneficial and economically viable
management of the world's forests.

For Ruth, Dan, Heath and Eckhart

*My, my, my! Such a lot of guns around town
and so few brains.*

—Humphrey Bogart, in
The Big Sleep (1946)

part one

1

Mr Timothy Greenhall looked very uncomfortable. I knew why. I'd spent money on the fittings of my Pyrmont office and he was sitting in a well-made chair with his feet on decent carpet and clean windows to look out of. He was facing a clean-shaven, recently barbered man in a fresh shirt sitting behind a desk that had only had one previous owner. True, there was no secretary or receptionist and if he was to get coffee or a drink I'd have to make it. But discomfort was built in—only a tiny percentage of people ever go into a private detective's office and they mostly wish they hadn't needed to.

'I deliberated long and hard before coming here, Mr Hardy,' Greenhall said.

I just nodded; nothing else to do with a statement like that.

Greenhall was a tidy-looking man in his late fifties or early sixties—neat grey suit, conservative haircut. He was thin in a way that suggested a disciplined life rather than athleticism. He took a deep breath as if he needed oxygen to fuel him for what he'd come to say.

'My son suicided five months ago.'

I still didn't say anything but I arranged my face in what I hoped was a sympathetic expression.

'Patrick was nearly thirty years old—the upper limit statistically for the cohort of young male suicides.'

Statistics? Cohort? I thought. *An accountant?* He hadn't mentioned his profession when he'd made the appointment earlier in the day by phone.

'You've done some research,' I said.

'A lot. I'm a businessman and I look very carefully at all the conditions and circumstances before I take any action.'

Again, I thought a nod would do.

'I know why Patrick killed himself. He was depressed; his affairs were in chaos, he was worried about his sexuality. We were . . . estranged.'

'That's a heavy load to carry.'

'Yes, and Patrick wasn't designed to carry heavy loads. He was what people call sensitive.'

I was getting a new fix on Greenhall. At first I'd thought he was a dry stick but his last sentence was charged with emotion. It was loving, critical and ironic all at once.

'Do you have doubts about whether your son suicided?'

'No, it was cut and dried. He shot himself through the temple.'

Greenhall surprised me again by demonstrating the action, right-handed with a cocked thumb and a pointed finger. He left the hand up at his head for what seemed like a long time before dropping it and giving a dismissive wave.

'He made a good job of it. For all his . . . youthful sensitivity and other problems he was an efficient person, like me. He liked things neat and tidy. Shit!'

He broke down then; his shoulders shook, sobs bobbed his head up and down and his eyes streamed with tears. He clenched his fists and babbled a muffled stream of swearwords with spittle flying from his lips. I got out of my chair to offer some help and he gestured for me to stay where I was. I pushed a box of tissues towards him but he took the handkerchief he had folded neatly in the top pocket of his suit coat and used it to blot his tears.

He lifted his tear-stained face. 'Do you have any children?'

'One, a daughter, and two grandchildren. Have you . . .?'

'Patrick was my youngest and his health was delicate in his early years. We spoiled him of course, gave him everything and . . . in the end, I suppose . . . nothing.'

I had to wonder where this was going. Seeing an apparently composed, even chilly, man break down wasn't something entirely new to me, but from what he'd said I couldn't see how I could be of use. Maybe he just needed to talk and I was wasting time and not making any money.

'That's being very hard on yourself, Mr Greenhall. I . . .'

He made a physical effort to pull himself together. He straightened his back and shoulders, shoved the damp handkerchief into a pocket and looked me in the eye. He'd made a remarkable recovery and now it was as if he'd never admit that he'd let himself go.

'I want to hire you, Mr Hardy, to find whoever it was who supplied my son with a gun.'

He was all manned-up now, tears wiped away and forgotten.

'And?' I said.

He smiled and there it was again, a complete change. He had a winning smile that reminded me of great actors like Rod Steiger and Jack Nicholson—a smile that won you over although you knew you didn't know exactly what it meant and couldn't trust it.

'I want you to kill him. Or her.'

2

Timothy Greenhall was a very wealthy man. He headed a company that made high-tech medical equipment and held a couple of patents for devices he'd invented which were used in operating theatres all over the world. He told me this after making his proposal and watching me shake my head.

'You're not serious,' I said.

He straightened his jacket and tie, which had got a bit rumpled. 'No, I just wanted to try to shock you but I see you're unshockable, which is good. Have you had such propositions put to you before?'

'And worse,' I said.

'All right. What I want is for you to find out who supplied the gun and see that the person is prosecuted to the full extent of the law. I imagine a pretty heavy sentence would be the result.'

'It'd be a toss-up,' I said. 'Assisting a suicide is a criminal offence but it's a dodgy area with voluntary euthanasia advocates in the mix . . .'

'I'm in favour of voluntary euthanasia.'

'So am I,' I said. 'So is almost everyone except gutless politicians and God-botherers, but you know what I mean. Lawyers can do all sorts of things when there's an ethical dimension to play around with.'

'What about possession of and supplying an unregistered gun?'

'That's a crime, certainly, but not exactly a hanging matter. Was the gun unregistered?'

'So the police said.'

'What sort of gun was it—rifle, pistol, what?'

'I've no idea.'

'You didn't see it?'

'No. I got a nearly hysterical . . . no, to be honest I shouldn't say that . . . an emotional call from Patrick's partner, but by the time I got to the flat the police were there and a swarm of other people. Patrick had been covered up and it was pandemonium. At the coronial inquest a police witness referred to an unregistered . . . weapon, I think he said, but I was busy comforting her—Alicia—and I scarcely followed the proceedings. If the make of the gun was mentioned I didn't take it in.'

After so long in the job, suspicion is an automatic reflex, and I had to ask what was a frequent question.

'Why have you come specifically to me with this?'

He told me he'd had business dealings with a guy I'd worked for a few years back on a case involving a shooting accident.

'I was told you seemed to know about guns and used police contacts in your investigation with some success. I thought you could be the man to handle this.'

'I'd have to probe into your son's life, talk to his partner and friends. I might turn up things you wouldn't want to hear.'

'He's dead. I'll never see him again. That's as bad as bad can be. People talk about closure. I always thought it was sentimental nonsense but I was wrong. That's what I want, closure. Call it revenge, if you like, I don't care.'

'There's nothing wrong with revenge.'

'I agree and I'm glad you think so. Will you help me, Mr Hardy?'

I was interested. Gun control was constantly in the news with drive-by shootings happening regularly and a conservative government trumpeting its law-and-order credentials while allowing amateur hunting in national parks. I had no liking for guns and regretted it every time I'd had to use one. I'd once thrown a pistol as far as I could out into Balmoral Bay and that pretty well summed up what I thought of firearms, but Greenhall's case presented interesting possibilities.

I had him sign my standard contract and he agreed to do an electronic transfer of a sizeable retainer to my bank account.

I got the full name of his dead son, the partner's name and her address. He'd worked as what Greenhall termed 'a sort of administrator' at the Powerhouse Museum in Sydney.

'What about friends?' I asked.

'I wouldn't know. I doubt if he had any, but his ... partner ... would be able to tell you that.'

He gave me the date of his son's death five months before, and said he'd stewed about the matter until he'd come to this decision. From memory, I'd been up in the Northern Territory on a case at around that time. I told him I hadn't seen any press reports of the suicide.

'It coincided with a couple of headline news stories,' he said. 'A big jewel robbery, I believe. That, and a major art scandal. What was it? A fake Old Master or the theft of a real one? I can't remember. We tried to keep the press, those that were interested, at bay, and not encourage the sort of lurid speculation that goes on in these matters.'

I got his details and told him I'd submit regular reports on my investigation by email.

'Last thing, your family. Do you have other children?'

'Yes, a daughter, Kate, unmarried. She lives at Mount Victoria in the Blue Mountains. She runs an organic plant nursery.'

He gave me her address and contact details but when I asked him what sort of terms the brother and sister were on he said he didn't know. The Greenhall family obviously wasn't harmony incorporated.

'Does your wife know you're intending to pursue this?'

He shook his head. 'She had a breakdown and she's under treatment at a facility in Nowra. Kate visits occasionally, I believe; she's got a big heart, Kate. I pay for it and I go when I can. This ... event helped to blow a fragile family apart, Mr Hardy.'

'Fragile?'

'Very. I worked like a slave, twenty-four seven, three hundred and sixty-five days a year to get my business established. I tried to make up for that with ... material things ... when I'd succeeded professionally and financially, but it was too late.'

He gave me the address of the Nowra clinic; we shook hands and I saw him to the door. He walked stiffly and held himself erect, like a man who was determined that nothing was going to tear him apart because he'd been there, suffered and survived, and had bolted himself back together.

I did the web searches you do as soon as the client is out the door. Greenhall's company, Precision Instruments Pty Ltd, had been the recipient of awards and commendations from the medical profession, export organisations and economists. It employed a large number of highly qualified people at a state-of-the-art laboratory and factory complex in Alexandria. Its stock price was high and several articles in professionally related magazines made the point that the company had prospered without government subsidy.

A trawl through the print media sites turned up coverage of Patrick Greenhall's suicide. An ambulance and the police had been called to a flat in Balmain, where a man had been found with a gunshot wound to the head. He could not be resuscitated. Names emerged over a series of low-key reports—Timothy Greenhall, Patrick Greenhall, his partner Alicia Troy. The coroner found that Patrick William Greenhall had committed suicide while the balance of his mind was disturbed. As the father had said, his son's death had low news value, especially with other more sensational things going on.

Unusually, there were no photos. It looked as though the Greenhalls' attempt to downplay the event had worked. Neither Alicia Troy nor Kate Greenhall came up in my search. The only discordant note raised was with the Nowra Revitality Centre, which had been investigated a few years back for having an unqualified doctor practising on the staff. Reading between the lines, it looked as though the place was a detoxification clinic.

I sat back and thought about what I'd learned. As always, the client never tells you the full story. 'Sensitive' could mean a lot of things—sexual, psychological, artistic. I'd been hired to discover some of the 'how' of Patrick's death but that was inextricable from the 'why'. It takes something powerful to compel you to shoot yourself; more flinch at it than succeed.

Hell is other people, someone once said. That's true in my experience, but it can be complicated. Hell can be the presence of other people or their absence. You can be alone in a crowd or a family or in a marriage.

I was going to have to talk to some of those physically present and perhaps emotionally absent people. Tricky territory, but at least I had one solid starting point—to find the provenance of the gun that had killed Patrick Greenhall.

3

Greenhall was right about me having police contacts. I'd carefully cultivated a few over recent years, getting back the relationships lost or strained in a couple of messy cases and making one or two new ones. Apart from my long-standing friendship with Frank Parker, formerly a Deputy Commissioner and now retired, these associations were always uneasy. Some were simply spin-offs from the friendship with Parker, a respected, even revered figure. Others were just what you might call drinking acquaintances.

It was now late on a Wednesday afternoon, a time when, like most people, cops are winding down and looking forward to their first drink. Some, no doubt, had already had their first, if not their second. I poured myself a glass of red wine and washed down some of the medication I'd have to take for the rest of my life after my heart attack and quadruple bypass. It wasn't the recommended way to take the pills but my cardiologist said red wine in moderation was good for the ticker. He didn't say anything about white wine, beer or scotch.

I had mobile numbers for the cops I knew and over the next hour or so, and two glasses, I got through to all but one of them with two simple questions: who would've been present following the Greenhall suicide and did they have any leads on who supplied the gun? The reactions surprised and puzzled me; none of them was willing to talk to me once I'd mentioned a gun. They pretended the call was breaking up or said they were busy and would call me back. It was a blue-and-white-checked dead end. Very frustrating.

I rang Frank Parker and got his wife, Hilde. I'd brought them together. I was anti-godfather to their son, Peter, and anti-grand-godfather to Peter's twins. Apart from my connection to my daughter Megan, her partner Hank and my grandsons Ben and Jack, it was my closest set of relationships, but one I'd neglected a bit lately in favour of my own family.

'Hello, Cliff,' Hilde said, her voice still German-accented after decades in the country. 'We've not seen you for some time.'

'Yeah, sorry, one thing and another.'

'You sound stressed. How's your heart?'

Fuck my heart, I thought, *just get me Frank*. But I said something polite and meaningless.

'Cliff,' Frank said when he came on the line. 'What's the trouble?'

'Why does there have to be trouble?'

'Hilde said you sounded stressed.'

'Just angry,' I said. 'I've been getting the runaround.' I took a deep breath and gave Frank an outline of what I'd been hired to look into and the reception I'd had from my police contacts.

'I didn't expect them to pour out their hearts, Frank, but I thought I might get a name or a point in the right direction at least.'

I heard what sounded like a long, exasperated sigh before Frank spoke again. 'Can't talk about this on the phone, mate. You'd better come over here.'

'When?'

'Soon as you can.'

It was getting late and with two sizeable glasses of wine inside me I didn't fancy driving to Frank's place in Paddington. I told him I'd be there mid-morning.

There are many things I'm unsure of, but I'm as sure as I know the sun will come up that Frank Parker never took a dishonest dollar in his forty years of police service. It just wasn't in his nature to do it, which is not to say that he'd always played by the book. In the old days he'd probably committed his share of physical violence and used threats and intimidation. His friendship with me hadn't helped his career but his honesty, energy and success rate had overcome that disability. In his retirement he was regularly consulted for advice by serving police.

I had these thoughts as I walked from Pyrmont to Glebe. I enjoyed the walk to and from the office on days I wasn't expecting to be driving anywhere, especially on a mild spring night like this. It gave me time to think and helped keep my weight down. The fish market was doing a roaring trade and I bought some dory fillets to cook for dinner.

I answered the knock at the front door at around 7 am. I'd slept for almost seven hours, pretty good these days, when I seem to sleep less than when I was younger. I was in pyjamas and a dressing gown and had been about to make coffee.

'Cliff Hardy?'

There were two men at the door. The one who'd spoken wasn't in uniform, the other one was and it didn't belong to the army, the navy, the air force or St John's Ambulance.

'Yes,' I said. 'Let's see the warrant card.'

He took out his wallet, flipped it open and held it close enough for me to read.

'Detective Sergeant Stuart McLean,' I read.

He pronounced it the Scottish way, '*McLain*'.

I looked over his shoulder, not hard to do because he was only about 175 centimetres tall and I'm 190. 'And you are?'

The uniformed man was tall enough to look me in the eye. 'Senior Constable Hawes,' he said.

'To what do I owe the pleasure?'

'We've come to inspect how you secure the .38 Smith & Wesson pistol you're licensed to own.'

'Secure?'

'That's right. You'll be aware of the regulation that requires you to keep the gun under lock and key and the ammunition similarly secured separately.'

'That's a tongue twister,' I said. 'Similarly secured separately . . . I'd have to say it slowly.'

McLean sighed. 'You're known for your pissy little jokes, Hardy. I have the authority to look at the gun.'

There was nothing else for it. I led them down the passage to the cupboard under the stairs and showed them where I kept the gun—zipped into a pocket of a leather jacket hanging deep in the cupboard. The .38 was fully loaded; I had ten bullets zipped into another pocket.

'Separate,' I said.

McLean almost smiled. 'But hardly secured. This is a serious violation. I'm confiscating the weapon and ammunition. You can apply to have it returned when you can demonstrate that you have two storing boxes, separately located.'

I shrugged. 'Sounds like a visit to Mitre 10. Well, I wasn't planning on shooting anyone today.'

With evident satisfaction McLean said, 'You'll find they're a speciality item and quite expensive.'

Constable Hawes produced a heavy plastic bag from a pocket and dropped the pistol and the bullets into it while McLean wrote out a receipt.

Hawes had a gruff bark but his manner, in contrast to

McLean's, was almost friendly. 'Combination or key lock, Mr Hardy. Your choice.'

I escorted them back to the door.

'Please don't say "Have a nice day",' I said.

McLean didn't even look back as he avoided the broken tiles on the path. 'Don't worry,' he said. 'I won't.'

'Quick work,' Frank Parker said when I told him about the visit later that morning. We were sitting outside near his small pool, drinking coffee. Frank was getting up from time to time to scoop leaves out of the pool with a net attached to a long pole.

'What's going on, Frank?'

He got up to do a scoop and to give himself time to think. He deposited the leaves in a box and came back to his chair and the coffee.

'It's one of those if-I-told-you-I'd-have-to-kill-you situations.'

'But you will tell me.'

'Reluctantly. Cliff, I know you have dealings with media people like Harry Tickener and trade information with them, but I'm serious—not a word of this to anyone, ever.'

I nodded. Frank was basically a very serious guy but what he'd said had struck a more than serious note, even for him. With a touch of warning about it.

'You know there's a lot of political pressure coming down about gun control. It's mostly bullshit but there are a few real problems. Handguns are coming in from unlikely sources, even from New Zealand, would you believe. A couple of the bikie gangs have established new chapters there and gun know-how is part of their recruiting procedure. Trading in guns makes them feel good. Apparently they get into New Zealand cheaply somehow from Eastern Europe and there's money to be made off-loading them over here. And now the network exists.'

'I didn't know anything about this.'

'You're not supposed to. That's the way the GC unit wants to keep it.'

'I'm guessing you mean a gun control unit,' I said. 'An undercover mob.'

'Yes and no. It has an undercover layer and a more public face, but some of its operations are completely covert.'

'That sounds very dodgy to me. What about account-ability?'

Frank didn't answer.

'So McLean and Hawes are part of the public face?'

'I'd say so.'

'But why would they target me? I was just making an enquiry about a piece of evidence connected with a sad event with no suspicious circumstances.'

Frank drained his cup, got up and went in pursuit of more leaves that had dropped from a tree with a branch that reached close to the pool. He performed the action he'd done a thousand times before with a long stroke and the flick of a wrist.

'I wish you'd stop doing that. Let the fucking Kreepy Krawly deal with the leaves.'

He shook the leaves into the box and sat back down. 'You are stressed.'

'I just don't like being targeted by the cops for a technicality. Okay, a careless mistake.'

'There's a special sensitivity about anything to do with the police and guns.'

'Now we're getting to it. Why?'

'The unit's had its problems, apparently. I'm not in the loop but I hear things. Questions have been asked about its . . . accountability, as you called it.'

'And that's all you'll tell me?'

'No, I'm also telling you to be careful.'

'It was a simple factual enquiry,' I said. 'It just needed a couple of simple answers. Are you saying that particular gun could have been . . . improperly disposed of?'

'I have no idea, but you're not the person to find out. You've been flagged, mate. You did a bit of time for destroying evidence—a gun—and you came very close to being prosecuted. You tried to shoot that bloke at Balmoral and chucked the gun in the bay.'

'I was upset then and I'm getting upset now.'

'Leave it alone. My sense is that it's political, which means dirty. All I know is that certain structures and people are under pressure.'

'Like who?'

He shook his head.

'Are you protecting your pension, Frank?'

He looked at me and I raised my hands defensively. 'I'm sorry. I didn't mean that.'

'Forget it. I didn't hear what you said. I'm getting old and deaf.'

4

Frank went back to scooping. I said my goodbyes to him and Hilde and left. I'd been warned off investigations before but usually by people on the wrong side of the law, not by those sworn to uphold it. I'd signed a contract to do something and I didn't like the idea of reneging on it. There were other people I could approach if I knew what type of gun Patrick Greenhall had used.

I knew an ex-stuntman and bikie, rendered paraplegic by an accident, who dealt in illegal guns. He knew others in the same game and their specialities. But without knowing whether the gun was a rifle or an automatic pistol or a revolver, I was flying blind at take-off.

I decided on a two-pronged approach. I went to the gun shop in George Street in the city and bought two combination-lock strongboxes. They came with lock bolts to allow them to be fixed to walls or floors. I cleaned out a kitchen cupboard. My handyman skills are limited but they were enough for me to be able to sink a couple of bolts through the gyprock into the masonry and fix the boxes side by side to the wall. Separated only by a few centimetres, but separated.

I called my lawyer, Viv Garner, told him the story and left him to contact the police about how to proceed in getting my pistol back now that I had the right set-up.

'If you have any problems, Viv,' I said, 'just let me know.'

'Problems? You? Okay, what problems? It's just a matter of . . . where were the police who took the bloody thing from?'

'I don't know.'

'You didn't ask?'

'They took me by surprise. I've got their names though.' I gave him the names.

'There's a bit of work in this,' he said. 'I hope you're getting paid.'

'I hope so, too.'

As I cut the call I had a fleeting thought that I might have exposed Viv to some danger or pressure. I dismissed the idea; he was a highly respected member of his profession and big in several legal associations. The only black mark against him was his association with me, which his colleagues put down to a touch of eccentricity. Viv said it pleased him to be provided with a spark of excitement in his otherwise dull, dutiful life.

*

I thought about the suicide of Patrick Greenhall and the people likely to have been present following it. The paramedics, uniforms and detectives, the SOCO until it was determined to be a suicide, and a police doctor. Not much chance of getting information from any of them, but there was one other person—Greenhall's partner. She'd found him and must have seen the gun. At the very least, no matter how upset she'd been, she should be able to tell me if it was a rifle or a handgun.

Greenhall Senior had given me her mobile number and I rang it. Five months was long enough to recover, I thought.

A crisp, educated voice. 'Alicia Troy.'

I explained who I was but left a little vague what it was I'd been hired to do. She listened without commenting. I said I'd like to talk to her.

'Why?'

I thought it best not to ask the crucial question bluntly. I said, 'To know more about Patrick, his habits, his movements. That's if you're willing to talk about it.'

'I am.'

'I have the address of Patrick's flat in Balmain. Are you—?'

'My flat, ours.'

'I'm sorry. Are you still there?'

'Yes. I'll be home from work by six-thirty. You could come then.'

'Where do you work, Ms Troy? Mr Greenhall didn't tell me.'

'He wouldn't. At the Powerhouse Museum. I was Patrick's boss.'

The flat was in Glassop Street near Elkington Park. Biggish block and if she was up high enough, Ms Troy would have a decent view of the water. Good security and an efficient lift, but second level at the back. View of houses and back yards only.

Alicia Troy surprised me. She was a tall, handsome woman with a good figure, dressed in a long horizontally striped blue and white skirt and a black sweater. She had abundant dark hair and a confident manner. She was also at least forty years old, probably more. She smiled when I failed to conceal my surprise.

'Expecting someone younger, Mr Hardy?'

'I was.'

She ushered me into a short passage that led to a large room. It was well appointed, with good furniture and appliances, but not what I'd anticipated for a presumably well-paid professional couple. She pointed to a corner where there was an arrangement of chairs around a small table.

'I'm drinking white wine. Would you like some?'

I said I would and forced myself to stop scanning the place, wondering where Patrick had killed himself. She came back with a bottle of Houghton's classic white and two glasses. She rucked up the long skirt she was wearing and settled herself into a chair opposite me across the table. The bottle was already open; she poured two large glasses.

She smiled. 'I can't stand being given a third of a glass,' she said. 'They know a person's going to need a top-up or two so what's the point?'

'I'm with you,' I said. 'They probably say too much affects the bouquet or something, but I'm more interested in the amount and the taste.'

We both took healthy swigs.

'So,' she said, 'poor Patrick. I have you at a disadvantage, don't I?'

'You have and I'm embarrassed. I know how old he was and I was told he was youthful-looking. So I made assumptions. I'm sorry. As you saw, I expected someone more Patrick's age. Not very imaginative of me. And this place—again, not what I thought.'

'It was my flat originally and he moved in about eighteen months ago. We smartened it up a little. Our tastes matched pretty much. We renegotiated the mortgage. I've changed things a bit more since he died.'

'What about his friends? Can you give me any names?'

'He didn't have friends,' she said, echoing Timothy Greenhall. 'Nor do I, really. We didn't need them. We were each *other's* friend.'

'Colleagues at the museum?'

'We never saw any of them after hours. In fact, he probably only ever talked to them at meetings. We all work hard on our own projects during the day, we don't sit around chatting in the coffee room.'

That sounded like a dead end, or at least something that could be put on the very back burner until I ran out of other ideas.

I asked a few more questions and she told me something about her relationship with Patrick. I sensed that it was an edited version, only natural since she was talking to a perfect stranger with no claims on her candour. She poured more wine and stopped talking.

'What are you thinking?' she said.

'I'm wondering why you're telling me so much. I know it's not everything, but I don't flatter myself I've won your confidence to this extent.'

Again, the smile. 'You surprise me, too, Mr Hardy. When you phoned, with that voice I imagined an ex-policeman, damaged by disillusion, booze and tobacco.'

I shook my head. 'I'm bruised a bit by those things but not too damaged. While we're being frank, you implied that Timothy Greenhall had reservations about the nature of your relationship with Patrick. Could you spell that out?'

'Can't you guess? His only son moving in with a divorcee nearly fifteen years older? And as for his wife . . .'

'Patrick's mother?'

'Yes, although you wouldn't know it from her behaviour. I'd be more inclined to doubt her maternity than his paternity.'

'What do you mean? *Was* there any question about Timothy being the father?'

'Patrick wondered, when he was depressed. Apparently Mr Greenhall made some cracks about it over the years, along the lines of "Well, you don't take after me, but I know why that is." '

She leaned forward. 'It's probably bullshit—I could see a lot of his expressions and mannerisms in Patrick—but Mr Greenhall's a very devious and manipulative man under that conventional exterior. He was probably needling Patrick's mother in some roundabout way. And she's even worse.'

I sat back, surprised at her vehemence; the chair creaked.

'I'm sorry', she said. 'The wine's making me garrulous and bitchy. It happens.'

I'd had enough of this. I wanted to shake her up a bit. I drank some wine and let my eyes drop to the dove-grey carpet. It looked new.

'Where did he do it?' I said.

'Over there near the window.' She pointed to the floor and to a large wall hanging. 'The blood hit the wall where that hanging is and there was quite a lot on the floor. I got a new carpet . . .'

She didn't break down the way Greenhall Senior had but there was a crack in her composure. I stood and crossed to where she said Patrick had stood. It had been at 6 am in winter and it would have been dark. He'd have been looking out at some house lights and streetlights, nothing more.

She'd collected herself while I stood there and her voice was steady. 'It's a funny thing but I feel I can talk to you and it's about time I talked to someone. We're supposed to be enlightened these days but I can tell you that a woman who takes up with a much younger man is in a kind of prison of disapproval. Turn around! Aren't you going to ask me if I loved him?'

I turned. Her fine-boned face was a mask of strain and stress.

'First I'm going to ask, where were you at six o'clock in the morning?'

I thought she might take offence but she didn't, or not seriously.

'Asleep. I'd worked late and I'm a very deep sleeper.'

'All right then, did you love him?'

'Yes, and there was nothing maternal about it, in case you're thinking . . .'

'I'm not thinking anything, Ms Troy.'

She straightened her shoulders and slowly allowed the tension to drain away from her face and body. She pointed to my half-full glass.

'Come and have some more wine. I'm sorry for the dramatics but I've had a hard time since Patrick's death. People have been ... solicitous, but there's often been something else behind what they say.'

I sat. 'What else?'

She raised her plucked eyebrows and I noticed for the first time how carefully she'd made up her face. She had high cheekbones, a long, straight nose and very full lips and had done everything possible to enhance those features and distract from the fine lines around her eyes.

She laughed. 'I suppose it's a mixture of "Well, he was just a toy-boy, what can you expect?" and "Mutton dressed up as lamb".'

'A twenty-nine-year-old isn't a boy. I don't even know what he really looked like. Was he good-looking?'

'Very.'

'I'd say he was lucky to have you.'

'Thank you.'

Neither of us spoke for a minute or so and then I pulled out my notepad, just as a prop. 'There was something I wanted to ask you. I wasn't sure if it was appropriate but I think now that it is. Did you see the gun Patrick used?'

'Yes, it was lying right beside him.'

'Can you tell me what kind of gun it was? Was it a handgun or . . .'

'It was a Glock G22 automatic.'

5

'You know about guns?' I said.

'Pistols,' she corrected. 'I know about pistols, rifles and shotguns. I worked at the Police and Justice Museum before the Powerhouse.'

'The Glock's a police weapon.'

'Not exclusively. I think you can buy one online if you know how to go about it.'

'Was it the standard model or the smaller one the plain-clothes guys use?'

'Now you're assuming it was a police pistol. I can't be sure. I was upset, as you can imagine. I know it was a Glock . . . the standard one, I think.'

I nodded and stood.

'You haven't finished your wine.'

'I have to drive.'

'You have to drive and I have to be fresh for work. Fair

enough. The dead have the power to cripple us but I'm not going to let that happen to me. I'm moving on.'

It seemed like an invitation to another question.

'Why did he kill himself, Ms Troy?'

'Because he only had brief periods of not hating himself.'

'Again, why?'

'I don't know.'

'Have you any idea how he got hold of the gun?'

She moved to steer me to the door. 'Try his mother; she despised him almost as much as she despised her husband and hated me. Goodnight, Mr Hardy.'

Driving home, I reflected that of course she was right—although it was widely used by police around the world, the Glock automatic was a commercial product and readily available. I knew it had a fifteen-shot magazine and an elaborate safety mechanism that meant it was unlikely to go off in your holster or if you dropped it. At a guess it would be expensive. I thought my bikie contact would know if there was anyone locally who specialised in Glocks, but Frank's implied reference to police and gun dealing couldn't be ignored.

Ben Corbett lived in a below-street-level flat in Erskineville. It was the sort of place that would've been flooded in the days when Erskineville was a slum area, but the suburb had undergone a big upgrading and Ben could now count on remaining dry in a Sydney downpour. He'd bought the flat when he was earning good money as a film and TV stuntman, part-timing as an outlaw bikie. A bike accident that should have killed him got him a compensation payout in return for life in a wheelchair.

Ben wasn't the kind of guy you phoned up for an appointment. You knew for almost certain he'd be at home and would see you if you had the right credentials—a packet of Drum tobacco and a bottle of Bundaberg rum. The following morning I equipped myself with these things and drove to Erskineville.

Someone had rigged up a pulley system that allowed him to haul himself up the too-steep ramp he'd had constructed from his flat to the street. It was a typical piece of Corbett bravado, along with refusing to have a motorised wheelchair. Wheelchairs are heavy and Ben weighed a hundred kilos plus, but he was one of the strongest men I knew and he could do it easily. He delighted in the challenge the ramp presented to his visitors and was notorious for the speeds he reached in his wheelchair on the street.

I walked cautiously down the ramp and knocked on the door. I heard swearing inside the small flat and the turning of wheels before the door opened.

'Hello, Ben.'

'Hardy, you cunt. What do you want?'

I held up the bottle and the now plain-packaged tobacco. 'Information, Ben. What else?'

'Not buying?'

I'd bought, or rather rented, a pistol from him when I'd needed one in my unlicensed period. I shook my head. 'Just a chat.'

'It'll cost you.'

'That's okay, I'm working.'

'Lucky fucking you. Come in.'

He spun the wheelchair around and scooted it across the room to where he had an electric fire burning. Mild outside, it was cold in the flat. He had the television playing and he muted the sound. A big ashtray on a table held the butts of his mid-morning rollies and he already had a streaked glass beside it.

'Coke's in the kitchen,' he said. 'Get yourself a glass and bring it in.'

'You seem almost glad to see me, Ben.'

'I'd be glad to see any-fucking-body except two of my three ex-wives.'

I knew what this meant but I played along. 'You make an exception for one of them?'

'No, she was a skaggy cunt, but she was on the bike with me and she's fucking dead.'

I went through to the grubby kitchenette, opened the fridge, got a bottle of Coca-Cola and took a reasonably clean glass from the draining board. I cracked ice cubes into a bowl and brought everything back to where Ben was sitting. I'd left the tobacco with him and he was already sniffing it suspiciously as I drew up a chair.

'What's the problem?' I said.

'It's this plain fucking packaging. You reckon it's the real stuff?'

I opened the rum, poured a solid slug into Ben's glass, added a little Coke and one ice cube. My drink was weaker but not too weak. I didn't want a macho tirade.

'Who knows?' I said. 'Some of the cigarette smokers put a coloured plastic case over the cancer warning.'

'Wimps,' Ben said. He rolled one from his existing packet, took a deep drag and let the smoke trickle out to contribute to the dark yellow stains in his bikie's beard and moustache. He took a heavy pull on his drink.

'So?'

'Glocks,' I said.

'What about 'em?'

'Do you handle them?'

'Fuck, Hardy, what sort of a question is that?'

'Come on, Ben, you know how we stand. I wouldn't dob you in, you've got too much on me.'

'I suppose that's right.' He sucked down smoke and rum. 'I wouldn't touch the fucking things. Too expensive and too easy to trace. Not a lot of them around.'

'So who does?'

He stared at me through the smoke. I'd been to the ATM; I reached into my wallet and fanned out five one-hundred-dollar notes like a poker hand.

'Not enough,' he said.

I added two more hundreds and a fifty. 'That's it.'

Ben took the money and slid it under his glass. He was a sloppy drinker and the wet glass left a ring on the topmost note.

'Dusty Miller,' he said.

'Where would I find him?'

'In the fucking Blue Mountains. He runs a smash repair place in Katoomba.'

'A chop shop?'

He shrugged. 'Could be.'

'I hope he's not a mate of yours, Ben. Not the sort of bloke you ring up and warn.'

'Are you kidding? He's a Bravado and I'm a Fink, or was.'

'Once a Fink always a Fink.'

'Are you taking the piss?'

'Just making sure.'

'He's an arsehole. I wouldn't give him a drink if he was dying of thirst. What's this about, Hardy? Do you need a gun?'

'No, I'm all legal now. I've got one.'

He nodded. 'Better be quick. Dusty's on borrowed time, so I've heard.'

'What d'you mean?'

He shook his head and I snatched the bottle away.

'Okay, okay. I don't know much about it but the word is Dusty's got an in with some cops and with all this shit going on that kind of fuckin' arrangement can only last so long. That's all I meant.'

I finished my drink, pushed the bottle back, and got ready to leave. Ben poured himself a refill.

'Hardy,' Ben said, 'd'you know anything about this stem cell stuff that's supposed to be able to fix spinal injuries?'

'Just what I read and see on the news, but we've probably got the wrong government now to move that ahead.'

'Fuck, is that right?'

'How did you vote in the last election?'

'I don't fuckin' vote. I'm an Enzedder, didn't you know?'

I moved to the door. 'Take care of yourself, Ben.'

He looked up from expertly rolling another smoke. 'Why're you saying that?'

'It's just an expression. I say it to everyone.'

I left and inched my way up the slope into a bright day and had to blink a few times to adjust to the light after the dimness of Ben's flat. I also needed a few breaths of fresh air to clear the atmosphere of smoke, booze, anger and despair.

It wasn't true that I used that expression all the time. If Ben had police contacts and everyone was so jumpy about guns, he was as much in danger as protected. And now there was a connection between him and New Zealand, where I'd been told guns were sourced. All his associations could be dangerous, and mine too.

Back at the office, the next thing on my list was Mrs Greenhall. I didn't feel like driving to Nowra on the off chance, so

I rang the Revitality Clinic to see if they had visiting hours over the weekend.

'Which guest did you wish to see?' asked the professionally smooth receptionist, who'd introduced herself as Tracy.

'Mrs Jillian Greenhall.'

'I'm sorry. Mrs Greenhall is not . . . encouraged . . . to have visitors at the moment.' The silky voice was very firm.

'And when *might* she be,' I imitated her telling pause, '"encouraged" to see people?'

I was told I could try again the next week to see if the situation had changed, and instructed to have a nice day. Another dead end, for the moment.

I spent what was left of the day catching up on paperwork, then went home with a takeaway curry and a nice bottle of white for dinner to go with the book I was reading.

6

I didn't much like the thought of fronting a Bravado bikie gun dealer, who ran what was possibly an illicit car repair business, without a weapon. I didn't have a gun so I went for the next best thing—money. Over the weekend I spent time in the gym and the pool at Victoria Park and made several visits to an ATM. When I set off on Monday morning I had a full tank of petrol and three thousand dollars. My Falcon was in very good condition but it was old and it'd be credible for me to claim it needed attention. At the very least I hoped to get a look at Dusty Miller and work out what to do next.

Like most Sydneysiders I'm ambivalent about the Blue Mountains. We're glad they're there but, with snow in the winter, searing heat in the summer and no significant sports venues, we feel it's a kind of foreign territory to be visited very selectively. The trick to driving there is to pick your time of departure. Anywhere around peak time and Parramatta

Road and the M4 can be a nightmare. The mountain road narrows after Emu Plains as you go up and is constantly under repair and upgrade. Eighty k is the rule for most of the way but it can drop suddenly to sixty through the towns and there are frequent forty-k school zones. Sneaky speed cameras are another hazard.

I left Glebe at eleven and encountered my share of the go-slows. There were still signs of the 2013 bushfires around Springwood, another factor that plays into our feelings about the mountains. We don't like hearing about the loss of lives and houses and we don't like the smoke that drifts down into the city.

I got into Katoomba just before one, with the heater working against the cold outside air. I was tired after the drive, eager for something to eat and ready for a drink to relax me and some coffee to spark me up. The Paragon café was the best source for all three. I took a seat, ordered shepherd's pie and peas with a glass of the house red. When the food and drink arrived I used the tomato sauce dispenser liberally. A Maroubra boy can't eat shepherd's pie without swamping it in tomato sauce.

I got directions to Miller's Smash Repairs from a waiter in the café.

'Won't be open until a good bit later,' he said.

'Why's that?'

'Dusty's a bikie, right? They roar off on Saturday arvo to do whatever it is they do and don't get back till late Sunday. Pissed, usually, so he doesn't open till late.'

I found the workshop at the end of a narrow street a few blocks back from the main drag. The street straggled through some low-grade housing until, once past the workshop, it became a track leading off into rugged bushland. A hand-painted sign identified it and oil stains on cracked concrete, a few rusty oil drums, some decaying batteries and an untidy pile of threadbare tyres confirmed the nature of the business. The junk also suggested neglect, if not indifference.

The fibro and weatherboard building had a long, low skillion at the back that looked like living quarters. It had a separate electrical connection from the workshop and a TV aerial. It was very quiet; none of the other houses in the street seemed to be occupied just then, and traffic noise from the main road was muted. Birds fluttered and called as I slammed my car door. I walked to the double doors of the workshop and rattled them, getting no response.

I had three thousand dollars in my wallet and a rolled-up newspaper in my hand. Inside the newspaper was a forty-centimetre length of lead pipe. I followed a path of poorly laid concrete blocks around to the side of the skillion. Twin small windows were too dirty to look through and a larger one further back had been broken and patched over with heavy cardboard.

There was a bricked sitting area at the back with some rickety chairs, milk crates filled with empty beer bottles and cans, and a few hubcaps doing duty as ashtrays. The back door was a ramshackle affair and had a broken panel mended with a sheet of thick Perspex. When I knocked on the solid part of the door there was no response. I waited. You don't go straight in after a no-response; you wait, watch and listen.

There was no sound from within or without other than the occasional bird call that seemed incongruously sweet and pure in that semi-derelict setting.

I was wearing a long-sleeved denim shirt under a corduroy jacket and I retracted my arm and used the shirt cuff to try the door handle. It turned easily and I pushed the door open with my foot. I eased into the room that served as a cooking, eating and smoking area. A leaf-cluttered skylight didn't do much against the dimness. The place was a mess, with chairs overturned, broken glass on the lino floor, a cupboard spilling food tins and packets, and clothes strewn about. The clothes smelled of urine and shit.

A half-open door led to another room and as I pushed at it I was hit by a familiar odour. People smell things differently. I've heard some say blood has a metallic reek, others speak of a chemical tang—maybe it depends on the blood. I was picking up the familiar acrid, raw smell I associated with a lot of blood fairly recently spilled.

The bedroom was the one with the dirty twin windows that let in just enough light to let me see something I hope never to see again. A big man lay on the bed. He was naked; his head had been virtually pulped; his long beard was blackened by blood, and a grey ponytail, tied with a leather thong, had been lopped off and stuffed into his mouth. Both earlobes were bloody and ragged where earrings had been torn away.

His pale, flabby body had bruises from shoulder to hip and dozens of burn marks that had bled and attracted flies. The bedding underneath him was sodden with blood, sweat and urine. I leaned against the doorjamb and fought a strong urge to throw up. This had to be Dusty Miller and the reason for his torture wasn't hard to guess—to find out where he kept the guns. It looked as though he'd held out for some time and I wondered if he'd given up the information. Hard to tell. The signs were that the torturer had lost control but it could've been he'd got what he wanted and then had had his fun.

I left the room, stepping carefully so as not to leave any boot marks or fibres or the hundred and one other things that forensics can use to place you at a crime scene. I exited the back room and pushed the door shut with my elbow. I worked my way slowly to the front of the building. My car, sitting there, suddenly looked to me like an advertising sign: HARDY WAS HERE!

I'd asked about Miller in the café. True, it had been busy, but would the waiter remember? I could have been seen driving to the workshop even though I hadn't noticed anyone around. Were the Falcon's tyre treads distinctive? Had I touched anything? I didn't think so but it was impossible to be sure.

Contacting the police wasn't an option. Frank had warned me that I'd been flagged as a gun-nuisance. It wasn't likely the cops would regard me as a suspect for Miller's murder, but the delays they could cause and the obstacles they could put in my path could just about take me out of business.

I needed time to think things through and since Patrick Greenhall's sister Kate was nearby in Mount Victoria, it made sense to stay in the area. But not in Katoomba when Miller was discovered. Mount Victoria was a safer bet.

7

The weather changed as I was driving to Mount Victoria. The sky clouded over and a cold wind had sprung up. People in the towns I passed through were hurrying, their hands buried in their pockets. I had trouble getting the image of the tortured and murdered man on the bed out of my mind. I'd never been subjected to anything that extreme, but I'd come close and I realised that I needed not just time to think, but some soothing peace and quiet around me. I booked into the Mt Vic Motor Lodge, not far from the railway station.

I keep my gym clothes—towel, sneakers and other bits and pieces—in a large overnight bag in the car, and that passed as luggage for the receptionist. I registered for one night and had no option but to use my credit card and enter my car registration number. If the police had information to follow up on me and looked north I was a goner, but I wasn't up to camping out in the bush.

There were eight or nine cars already parked and another drove in as I was registering, making it less likely the busy receptionist would take any notice of me. The place boasted an extensive garden, a swimming pool, still covered, and views of the high country surrounds. The room was cold and I turned the air conditioner up to its warmest level.

I'd prepared for the mountains by bringing the fully lined parka in which I'd kept my gun and ammunition until Detective McLean had come to call. I put it on and walked down the town's main street, where I bought bread, cheese, a tomato, mustard, a bottle of merlot and a packet of disposable razors. The wind had a keen edge that suited my mood. I walked for the best part of an hour, not thinking much, just trying to put time and distance between myself and a man who'd died the hard way.

The room was too warm when I got back and I adjusted the heat level. I opened one of the light beers from the mini-bar and settled into a chair with that and a packet of crisps and waited for the 5 pm television news, like a cinema-goer waiting with popcorn for the feature. Sitting and waiting in motels was something I'd done hundreds of times all over the country. It had the effect I wanted; it made me feel normal, almost.

Dusty Miller had made the news. The police had kept the media back but the scene was dramatic enough with police cars, an ambulance and about fifty Bravados swarming around the old workshop. The reporter announced that one of Miller's mechanics had found him when he turned up for work at two-thirty, the usual Monday opening time. He'd contacted the authorities and also the bikies, being a Bravado himself. As usual, this information was followed by a whole lot of wild speculation that linked Miller to unspecified crimes. The police appealed to anyone with information to come forward. Good luck with that.

I watched a few of the other news items before switching the set off and laying out the bread, cheese, tomato and mustard and opening the wine. I carved chunks off the small, crusty loaf with my Swiss Army knife and used the motel's crockery, cutlery and glassware for the meal. As I ate and drank I wondered why I'd used my own money to buy the food and hadn't had a restaurant meal I could charge to Timothy Greenhall. I was halfway through the bottle when I knew the answer: it was one of those few times when I had doubts about becoming a private detective—discovering dead bodies, dealing with desperate men and women and all that associated sadness. I could have stayed in the army, or persisted with the law degree or even turned pro as a boxer.

Useless, and I shook the feeling off. I seemed to have stumbled onto something very dark, where people were prepared to go the limit. Had Dusty Miller supplied the gun that killed Patrick Greenhall? I'd never know, but if he had, it was odds-on he was killed by someone out there who'd done business with him, and the police, like me, were going to try to find out who Miller's clients were. That is, some of the police. What about the others? If there was a rogue police gun-dealing crew, already alerted to me, aware somehow that I'd been in Katoomba around the time of Miller's death, I'd have to lock all my doors and sleep with a gun, which I didn't have, under my pillow.

I realised I was building a paranoiac scenario but I let it build. What if *they* hadn't discovered Miller's guns and thought I *had*? And what about the bikies? I finished the food and most of the wine and used the motel's instant coffee. I spiked the coffee with scotch from the mini-bar and tried to watch a film on the television that consisted of such quick cutting, men who mumbled and women with such chirpy New Jersey accents who all looked the same that I couldn't understand what was being said or what was at stake. I chased across the channels for news but learned nothing more about the dead Bravado.

I checked the lock on the door, wedged a chair under the handle, stripped to my underwear and got into bed with my lead pipe for company.

In the morning I showered, shaved with difficulty using soap and a disposable razor, and ate breakfast in the motel dining room. Politics and football had pushed Dusty Miller lower down the news list but there was one item of interest: an unnamed Bravado veteran said the club would do whatever it took to find out who'd killed their 'brother'.

I used my laptop to locate Kate's Organic Nursery. It turned out to be a short distance from the township in an area divided into one-hectare blocks looking out over a valley to the Bell's Line of Road. I checked out and drove there along a recently built road past weekenders, A-frames and log houses, until I reached the nursery. A tasteful sign announced it and a curving gravel approach ran through flowerbeds and shrubberies to a low-lying timber and glass building painted in muted colours that blended with the surroundings and the rocky cliff that rose up at the back of the block.

There was space for about six cars to park but the only vehicle there was a Land Rover. A tarpaulin-covered trailer stood next to it. The air was crisp and cold but the sun was up with the promise of some warmth later. The main building was flanked by a large greenhouse, where I could see some movement. I approached it and knocked on the metal-framed glass door. A woman inside straightened up from whatever she'd been doing and beckoned to me. I opened the door and stepped into a colourful combination of plants and scents that seemed to belong to another world.

The woman came towards me. She was tall and heavily built, wearing overalls and an apron and carrying a trowel. She also had on boots, gloves and a woollen watch cap with wisps of dark hair poking out. She stripped off the right glove as she approached.

'Mr Hardy,' she said. 'I've been expecting you.'

I shook her strong, work-hardened hand. 'Your father told you about me.'

'That's right. I'm Kate Greenhall . . . obviously.'

'I've come to talk to you about your brother—again, obviously.'

She smiled, showing white teeth in a weather-beaten, freckled face that was disfigured by a pale, puckered scar running down her right cheek. It was the sort of mark skilful makeup could at least partly have concealed, but her face was scrubbed clean.

'I have to finish a few things here, then I'll be with you. Would you like to go into the house and wait? I won't be long.'

'Okay, thanks.'

Turning away, she said, 'Are you interested in flowers, Mr Hardy? Or organic gardening?'

'Not in the least,' I said.

She laughed. 'Honest. I like that.'

When people invite you to enter their premises unaccompanied they either have nothing to hide or, if they do, they're sure you won't find it. I went into the house, which featured polished pine floors with rugs and serviceable furniture. The sitting room's brick fireplace was laid but not burning; the house was warm from some other heating source. I browsed the bookshelves, mostly stocked with books about botany and gardening. The CDs were all classical. The hallway had several abstract paintings on the walls that could have been originals, and good, for all I knew. The place had a spartan but moneyed feel.

A few magazines, again with flowers on the covers, and the morning's local paper lay on a coffee table in front of the fireplace. Dusty Miller occupied the whole of the front page. In the centre was a photograph of him astride his Harley. With the beard, the ponytail, the sleeveless denim shirt, the studded belt and the leather vest he looked formidable despite the beer fat. It must have taken two or maybe three people to bring him down. I dropped my card onto the paper.

'Our little bit of underbelly,' Kate Greenhall said. I hadn't heard her come in and turned to see her without her apron and boots. 'I'm expecting a spike in sales.'

'How's that?'

'The bikies'll lay on a massive funeral, thunderous, and flowers galore.'

'You're a florist as well as a nursery?'

'Yup, I supply a shop in Katoomba. Come out to the kitchen. I'll make coffee and we can talk.'

I waved my hand. 'What about your business here?'

'Didn't you notice? There's a button by the greenhouse door. I can hear the bell anywhere on the block.'

I followed her through to a kitchen with the same feel as the living room—stylish practicality. She gestured for me to sit at a pine table while she worked at an intricate-looking coffee machine. In her socks she stood about 180 centimetres and I'd have guessed her weight at about eighty kilos.

I realised I was evaluating her physically as if she was a man. There was something asexual about her and it was more than the watch cap and the overalls.

A strong coffee aroma suddenly filled the room and she grinned when she saw my reaction.

'Good, isn't it? I'm a coffee purist. You only get it black here and you can't sugar it. Metal should never touch coffee, did you know that?'

I shook my head. 'Do you grow it?'

'I wish, but it's just a bit too cold up here. I get the beans from an impeccable source and I only grind what I immediately need.'

She poured the coffee into two ceramic mugs, brought them to the table and sat across from me with her legs splayed out. She blew softly at the mug and took a sip. I did the same. The coffee was rich and smooth, tasting as good as it smelled, rare with coffee.

'What d'you think?' she said.

'I could almost give up wine and whisky.'

She laughed. 'No, you couldn't. Right, now for poor Paddy.'

'Paddy?'

'That's what I called him. I was three years older and he was a pompous little boy and I called him that to take him down a peg or two.'

'Were you fond of him?'

'I loved him dearly, even after he did this to me.' She touched the scar on her face. 'He came at me with a knife when he was high on crystal meth or something. We hushed it up. He went into detox and therapy afterwards.'

'Why did he kill himself, Ms Greenhall?'

'I don't think he did.'

That rocked me. If she was right it added a new dimension to the troubled life of Patrick Greenhall and would affect my approach to the case from here on. I took a strong pull on the coffee and felt its effect on me, sharpening my responses to everything around me—the bird calls outside, the humming of the refrigerator, the lingering smell of the ground beans.

'That's the first time I've heard anything like that. The police were satisfied.'

She shrugged. 'The police are easily satisfied when they want to be. A man with a history of drug abuse and mental disturbance, working in a job well below his capacities and living with an older woman, is easy to write off.'

'Do you have any evidence?'

'Patrick told me he was in fear of his life because of something he'd seen.'

'Seen? What?'

'He wouldn't tell me.'

'What did you do about it?'

She drained her coffee mug and clenched her big hands around it. 'Nothing. I just assumed Patrick was back on the drugs and paranoid. I told him to go back into therapy and he got annoyed and we had a quarrel.'

'When was this?'

'A week before he died. D'you want some more coffee?'

I said I did and watched her as she went through the process again. She was an odd mixture of strength and fragility. She seemed to be one of those people who immerse themselves in practical activities to avoid introspection; a bit like me, or so I've been told.

She rinsed the mugs, dried them carefully and refilled them. She put them back on the table and leaned forward.

'I kept quiet about what Patrick had said because I was waiting for something to happen, and now it has.'

'And that is what?'

'You.'

'I don't understand.'

'I don't think my father really cared about who supplied the gun. What he really wants is for you to find out who killed his son and why.'

I thought back over the interview with Greenhall. I'd had the sense that he hadn't told me everything but that's nearly always the case anyway. With those misgivings aside, I'd been convinced that his commission for me was as he'd laid it out. If his daughter was right, I'd completely misread him. I resisted that idea.

'That wasn't my impression,' I said. 'Why wouldn't he just come out and ask me to investigate his death?'

'I don't mean he *consciously* wanted that. He's a mass of denials, guilts and insecurities. Deep down he suspects . . .'

'What?'

'That Patrick's death has something to do with the only thing he really cares about.'

'And what's that?'

'His precious bloody business.'

I thought about that as I drank the strong, flavourful coffee. Kate Greenhall sat quietly drinking her own and seemed content to let me cogitate.

After a few minutes a noise like an air-raid siren sounded and she jumped up and left the room. I was suddenly becoming aware of the cold and I assumed the central heating had a time switch. Sunlight flooded in through a window. A nice day in the Blue Mountains, except that it was turning out to be a puzzling one.

She came back rubbing her hands.

'The Bravados?' I said.

'No, an order for shrubs to make a hedge and I get to do the planting. Where were we?'

'That Patrick's death had something to do with your father's business.'

'Before we get back to that, I assume you've spoken to Alicia Troy?'

'Yes,' I said. 'Why?'

'What did you think of her?'

'I hadn't thought one way or another. She seems okay.'

'My mother hates her like poison.'

'That seems to be mutual.'

'I'm on Alicia's side there—my mother is poison.'

'What's the nature of her illness, if you don't mind me asking?'

'I don't much and I suppose you'd find out anyway. Call it alcoholism combined with nymphomania and fetishism. She had a thing for uniforms that eventually got out of hand.'

Psycho city, I thought. 'So what did Patrick's death have to do with your father's business?'

She looked uncertain for a moment. 'I don't know, really. Just a couple of cracks Patrick made about dirty money. He didn't tell me any details.'

'But you think your father really wants me to investigate whether Patrick was murdered, not just who supplied the weapon?'

'Right. I don't envy you working for him, Mr Hardy. He's a very complex and devious man.'

The second time someone had told me that. I was starting to think they might be right.

part two

8

I drove through Katoomba and its environs with the care of someone down to his final penalty points. Thankfully I wasn't but the last thing I needed was to register my presence there with the police. The town was quiet, though I imagined the Bravados were making plans to change that big time.

To say I was confused would be an understatement. I prided myself on being, if not a great judge of character, then at least a better than average one, due to a lot of experience. I hadn't judged Timothy Greenhall to be the complex and devious character his daughter said he was. Could she be right? I kept thinking back to the scene in the kitchen. The big, almost mannish woman with her air of detachment had exhibited a feeling of being involved in something else, something deeper than mere suicide or murder. Above it all, almost untouched by it, but seeing it clearly.

I had two women judging a third to be poison and one of those women judging the other to be the same. Over the years, I'd developed a habit of mentally seeing the people in whatever case I was working almost as actors in a play. I couldn't get a grip on the character of Patrick Greenhall. Was he a lost soul experimenting with drugs and clinging to an older woman for survival, or a player in some deep game to do with his business-obsessed father? I was used to judging people by their actions and the man had either shot himself or been shot. Big difference.

I stopped in Medlow Bath for lunch and to check my phone for calls and texts. I'd had the thing switched off since the night before. I still disliked the technology and resisted letting it dictate my movements the way some people do. There was nothing that required my immediate attention.

I left the mountain road and had to concentrate on the more complex traffic through the outer suburbs. I played Van Morrison's *Astral Weeks* for mental relief, something beautiful and meaningless. I tried to shake off the confusion and make plans. Ring Harry Tickener at the *Sentinel* and try to learn more about Greenhall and Precision Instruments; go through the legal hoops to recover my pistol; tot up my expenses and act like a professional. These practical, manageable things were steadying me as I parked the car more or less outside my house.

A spring shower broke just as I left the car. With my keys and a plastic bag holding the bread, mustard and cheese

I hadn't eaten in one hand and, in the other, the lead pipe I intended to put back with other junk in the courtyard, I walked up the path, avoiding the broken tiles and with my head lowered against the rain. A figure rose up from the gloom of where the porch was shadowed by overgrown shrubs.

'Hardy . . .'

The voice was harsh, threatening, and my nerves were still on edge. Acting on instinct I swung the pipe in the direction of the threat and felt it hit solid flesh.

'Christ.' The voice was thinner now and I was almost knocked off my feet as the very big man in a police uniform collapsed.

Senior Constable Hawes was stunned but not concussed or seriously injured. His cap and thick curly hair had absorbed much of the impact and he seemed to be blessed with a strong neck and a hard skull. I helped him inside, sat him down and got him some paracetamol and a glass of water. He swallowed the pills, blinked a few times and handed back the glass.

'How do you feel?'

'Foolish,' he said. 'Do you always have a blackjack in your hand?'

'You were unlucky. I'm sorry.'

'My fault. I should've been more careful.' He put his hand

to the side of his head, took it away and examined it. 'No blood. No harm done.'

'This is weird, if you don't mind me saying so. What the hell are you doing here and why isn't your first action to arrest me for assault?'

'Because I need your help. Tell you what, to square us up I could do with a drink.'

So could I. I gave him a choice of wine or whisky and he chose the whisky. We moved to the kitchen and sat opposite each other at the bench with big measures of scotch and the bottle of Bell's and a bowl of ice within reach. He stuck out a big, freckled hand.

'Colin Hawes.'

We shook. 'Senior Constable,' I said.

'Acting Sergeant.'

'Congratulations.'

He almost winced. 'Don't know for how long.'

It took him quite a while and a fair bit of whisky to tell his story, but the long and the short of it was that he had evidence that some former members of the GCU had been, and still were, involved in precisely what they had been commissioned to stamp out—illegal importation and sale of firearms.

'And worse,' he said.

'Such as?'

'You have to understand that this isn't serving members of the force. When the unit was set up it included civilians and a few retired cops—consultants, researchers and such. At first the unit had a green light.'

'Why?'

'The politicians were panicked about terrorism. No, that's not it; they were spooked by the shock jocks and the tabloids; they worried about being seen as not doing anything about it. The unit was bloody window-dressing, a response to that perception rather than to anything real.'

'How could that work? I thought it was supposed to be covert.'

'There's covert and covert. Certain operations were made more or less public. The pollies could hint that they were . . . taking the right steps.'

He sighed and rubbed at the side of his head. His pale blue eyes looked tired and strain showed in the tightening of his jaw and the way he looked at his almost empty glass. I offered him more scotch but he shook his head.

'Things got out of control. Some of the people in the unit crossed the line—they harassed people who had some clout. They took pay-offs. There was a shake-up and sackings and resignations.'

Reminiscent of the Armed Hold-up Squad, which had green-lighted armed hold-ups, I thought. 'So far, so good,' I said.

'Yeah, but now there's a group who used to be in the unit running a racket that involves not only guns and bribes and protection, but other things—corruption of customs officers, providing guns to crims, financing drug deals and lots of other stuff.'

'If it's known who they are they should be easy to crack down on. And if they're no longer police, why the big problem?'

'It's not so simple. They know too much and there's a massive cover-up going on. If it all came out about the shit things the unit did back when it had a free rein, the stink would spread across the whole force. So they've got some high-level protection. Not collaboration exactly but . . . policy at a pretty high level . . . call it damage control.

'It's getting to be a problem for me. I can see it happening and honest cops are getting drawn into it. The answer to your question, Hardy, and the reason I'm here is the same—because of former Deputy Commissioner Frank Parker. An enquiry you made about a gun was logged and that's what sent McLean here to check on where you kept your weapon. Everyone knows you're tight with Parker and I reasoned you'd ask him about the . . . harassment.'

'You were right.'

'I guessed he'd tell you something about the GCU, not too much.'

'Right again.'

'He wouldn't know what's going on. It's a bad scene, Hardy, and big. The people I'm talking about are tied in with a few politicians and political advisers and some shonky lawyers. There's a lot of money involved and a lot of careers and reputations.'

Cop cover-up, I thought. *I don't need this.* 'McLean seemed like an all-right guy.'

'McLean's a good example. He does what he's told.'

'If you know all this you should be talking to ICAC.'

He shook his head. 'You know what happens to whistle-blowers. Have you ever seen one in the police come out on top? There's an unspoken system for managing dissidents. I've got some evidence but I acquired it illegally. That fact can be manipulated, as you can imagine. The thing is, this kind of cover-up is corrosive and it spreads. For example, I'm sure someone involved has his eye on me and I've been promoted to keep me sweet. That worries me. I've got the feeling I'm being watched. I don't feel happy about going home. You're vulnerable at home in all sorts of ways.'

'I can see how that would worry you, but what do you want me to do?'

'Set up a meeting with Parker. If I can convince you I've got something serious to say we can both convince Parker. I don't know him, you do. The word is you have . . . influence with him.'

'I wouldn't say that. We've done favours for each other from time to time.'

Hawes's voice took on a desperate tone. 'Look, I'll make a statement to him and produce the evidence. He's an absolute cleanskin—no baggage—one of the few at that level. He should be able to . . .'

'Do what?'

He shrugged. 'Something . . . Look, there's someone else involved in this with me. I . . .'

He suddenly sagged sideways. Colour drained from his face and he closed his eyes briefly before straightening himself and reaching for his glass.

'Sorry,' he said, grinning. 'Stress, plus your blackjack.'

I thought Hawes was manipulative. It didn't mean he wasn't genuine.

'I have to think about this,' I said. 'Can I reach you tomorrow?'

He tossed off the last of his drink and the expression on his big, plain face was troubled. 'I'm not sure. I've got nowhere safe to go.'

I offered him the spare room for the night and he accepted. The bed was already made up. I gave him a towel and I heard him shower and close the door. It was early to go to bed but he looked all in. I was tired myself but I hadn't had to wrestle with his problems and I hadn't been hit on the head with a lead pipe.

I spent the rest of the evening making a few notes on what I'd learned during the day and constructing one of my diagrams connecting up people and facts in boxes, joining them with solid or dotted lines according to the value of the connection. It sometimes helped.

I wasn't hungry but I had heart medication to take and I'd learned not to take it on an empty stomach. I finished off the bread and cheese from the night before and washed the pills down with the bit of wine still left. My thoughts were scattered: I wanted to ask Hawes if he had any information on the Dusty Miller killing but that meant trusting him a bit further than I was willing to go. I thought I might show him the locked boxes I'd installed just for fun. And that was such a silly idea I knew I'd done all I could usefully do that day.

After a lot of driving, whisky and wine I slept soundly. I got up feeling a bit frowsy, thought about making coffee and knocked on the spare room door. No answer. I opened the door to an empty room, with the bed neatly made and the damp towel spread on the back of a chair. I went downstairs and found a note anchored by the whisky bottle on the bench. A newspaper and a magazine had been pushed aside to make room for a sheet of notepaper. Slanted block capitals:

THANKS, HARDY. THERE'S SOMETHING I HAVE TO DO. I'LL GET BACK TO YOU. HAVE THIS FOR FREE—YOUR CLIENT'S INVOLVED IN THIS. GUNS ARE PRECISION INSTRUMENTS. CH

9

It's an uncomfortable thing to discover that not only has your client held back information but that he or she may be culpably involved in the very matter you've been commissioned to investigate. There seemed no reason why Hawes would lie to me and it was impossible to ignore his statement. Clearly, I needed to find out more about Greenhall's business before I confronted him with the information.

Harry Tickener has a lot of people feeding information to him for his newsletter—from players, managers and journalists with the good oil on a variety of sports to political insiders and financial analysts. I emailed him asking for an appointment to discuss Precision Instruments. Harry usually gets back to me quickly but I was impatient and rang his office and made the appointment for that afternoon. My phone rang immediately I finished the call.

'Cliff, Viv.'

'Shoot,' I said.

He groaned. 'I wish you wouldn't do that.'

'No you don't, it makes your day.'

'Stop it. Ring Acting Sergeant Hawes and make an appointment for someone to inspect your gun security. Here's the number.'

He read it off and I wrote it down with a feeling of disbelief that must have been apparent when I thanked him.

'You sound edgy. What is it now?' he said.

'It's complicated.'

'What else is new? I have to go. I'm briefing a barrister named Paul Salmon who charges two thousand an hour and if you call him a big fish I'll never speak to you again.'

'I owe you, Viv.'

'You certainly do.'

He cut the call and I sat there looking at a screen that pinged twice and threw up two messages—one from my server offering me an upgrade and one from my daughter to tell me that my grandson Ben had a hard question for me. I didn't need an upgrade and I had all the hard questions I could handle.

I rang the number Viv had given me and got a voice message in Hawes's distinctive gruff tones.

'You've reached City Command. Please leave your number and your call will be returned.'

Which told me precisely nothing. Was Hawes in the wind or was he in the ground? I left my mobile number.

I rang Megan and told her I was busy but that I was looking forward to Ben's question.

'Give me a hint what it's about,' I said.

'What d'you reckon? Dinosaurs, of course.'

'I know bugger-all about dinosaurs.'

'Better mug up. The Wikipedia entry runs to about twenty pages. Eighty footnotes, from memory. Good luck.'

I drank two cups of strong coffee and listened to the ABC news station. Dusty Miller didn't figure; storms in various parts of the world did. Two drive-by shootings in the western suburbs got a mention. The phone rang and I answered it.

'This is Constable Cathy Carter from City Command, Mr Hardy. Returning your call.'

'I was expecting Acting Sergeant Hawes.'

'He's on leave. I assume this is to do with your weapon.'

I told her that I'd installed locked boxes and she said an officer would contact me to make an appointment to inspect the security.

'When?'

'I really can't say.'

'That's not satisfactory.'

'Are you anxious to recover the weapon, Mr Hardy?'

'I don't think that's an appropriate question, Constable.'

She realised she'd made a mistake and sounded flustered. 'You'll be advised of the time.'

I thanked her but I was speaking to a dead line.

I went to the gym and threw myself into an ambitious

routine. Wes Scott, owner, trainer and philosopher, came up as I was drooping sweatily over the sitting bench press. He took my towel and fastidiously wiped down the equipment. He'd greyed up over the years but hadn't put on a gram of fat, a reproach to us all.

'Cliff,' he said, 'what gives, my man?'

' "I gotta world of trouble on my mind." '

'Middle of the road in my humble opinion. Pulling a muscle ain't going to help now, is it?'

'What do you suggest?'

'What I always do—talk to a friend, if you have one.'

Harry Tickener was a friend of long standing and when I turned up at his Darlinghurst office in the late afternoon he already had some notes scribbled ready for me and two stubbies of low-carb beer. We screwed the tops off and touched bottles.

'To the new century,' he toasted.

'Shit, Harry, we're well into it.'

'I need to slow it down, it's going too fast. Don't you feel that? Don't you get to Saturday and think how can it be Saturday again already?'

'Sometimes I do; sometimes I think it can't come soon enough.'

'There speaks a man who has variety in his life. Enviable. Get those hops into you.'

'Do they still use hops to make beer?'

'I haven't the faintest fucking idea. You've bowled up an interesting one here, Cliff. Give me the drum.'

That was the way we operated. When I enlisted Harry's help I first had to tell him almost everything about the case I was working on. He accepted that it wasn't for publication and on his part he didn't tell me more than he judged I needed to know about his sources.

I outlined the Greenhall matter and some of its twists and turns—the apparently mutual antagonism between the women, the suspicion that Patrick Greenhall hadn't suicided and the suggestion that Precision Instruments might not be the squeaky clean operation it was supposed to be.

'That's a very bad pun, even for you.'

'Unintentional.'

'Nothing's unintentional with you, mate. I learned that a long time ago. Why the stress?'

That was Harry; he always probed for more and I always gave it to him. 'Police involvement.'

'Right, understood. Well now, Tommy Greenfall and Precision Instruments.'

'Tommy Greenfall?'

'That's what he was called when he came fourth in pistol shooting at the 1980 Olympics.'

'Is that a fact?'

'It's a little known fact. Do I go on?'

I nodded and took a long swig of the beer. It suddenly tasted more interesting.

Harry consulted his notes. 'With the US out of the picture, the Moscow games didn't get the attention the Olympics usually attract and no one really cares about who comes fourth anyway. But there was a whisper in pistol-shooting circles . . .'

'Be hard to hear a whisper in those circles.'

'Fuck off. A whisper that Tommy had modified his pistol illegally. It got hushed up but he never competed again. He changed his name slightly, got first-class honours in engineering at UNSW and the rest is history. From your expression and the fact that you've stopped drinking, I gather this is interesting.'

'Right. What do they whisper in finance circles where they can be heard above the clicking of the keys?'

'This 'n' that, but it's a long time ago, and there doesn't seem to be any info on how he got his start-up capital, which is always the tricky thing, as you and I know from not having had any to speak of.'

'And now he's riding high with profitable patents and exports.'

'Yes and no. A couple of the patents are being challenged in the US, where they make a business out of such things, and the exports are very high value, which gave him a surge. But volume's not that great and there's strong competition from places that don't play by the rules.'

As two who didn't always play by the rules ourselves, we toasted each other with more beer.

'I hasten to add,' Harry said, 'that there's an element of speculation in this. There's a kid doing a PhD on how some big, medium and small companies survived the GFC. He says Precision Instruments is only a footnote, but there's something curious about it.'

'Curious or suss?'

'He reckons you don't use judgemental terms in an economics thesis in case one of your examiners has a vested interest.'

'As befits someone in a three-piece suit.'

He almost choked on his beer. 'You only make jokes that bad when you're unsure of what you're doing.'

'You're absolutely right. I'm going to have to tackle Greenhall directly and I don't know what to say to him. I'm possibly going to talk myself out of a job.'

'Leaving you with a lot of unanswered questions.'

I nodded and finished the beer. 'Is there anything else, Harry?'

'One more thing. Greenhall's wife is from money but it was all in a family trust. She got income from it but no access to the principal, so she couldn't provide any of the initial capital. Also, she couldn't have helped him through the GFC if he had problems then.'

'Why not?'

'She was a drunk by then and the family had tightened the strings—practically cut off her money supply altogether.'

My mobile rang as I was leaving Harry's office and Constable Cathy Carter told me she would call at my house at 5 pm to inspect my security arrangements.

'If that's convenient,' she added.

'What if it isn't?'

'Then there could be a considerable delay. With Acting Sergeant Hawes on leave, work is piling up.'

I said the time was convenient and got back to Glebe with half an hour to spare. I tidied the kitchen and then untidied it by making coffee and eating some rice cakes with French mustard and cheese. I'd skipped lunch and Harry's beer had woken an appetite. From the sound of her, Constable Carter wouldn't be all business and wouldn't care if I had dishes in the sink. The doorbell sounded when my coffee was half drunk.

She was small and would barely have met the height requirement for police back when that still operated and wasn't considered discriminatory. I tried not to loom over her as I escorted her through the house. She had a soft briefcase under her arm that seemed to have a bit of bulk to it. I offered her coffee and she refused. She put the briefcase down on the kitchen bench with a clunk.

'Okay, let's have a look.'

I opened the cupboard and showed her the boxes. I'd memorised the combination and opened them.

'Should help the resale value,' I said.

'That's a joke, is it?'

I closed everything up. She was opening the briefcase and putting documents on the kitchen bench. I noticed then that her shoulders sagged, either with tiredness or something else. In someone so small to start with it sparked sympathy in me.

'Sorry for the lousy joke. I know it's a serious matter and I'm happy to comply with the regulations. If I have.'

She sighed. 'You have, Mr Hardy. To tell you the truth I think it's anachronistic for PIAs to be licensed to own weapons at all, but that's for others to decide.'

'I'm inclined to agree with you.'

She gave me a surprised look. 'If you'll just sign these papers I'll return the pistol and ammunition and I'll trust you to lock them away.'

I reached for my coffee mug on the bench, pushed away an insert from a magazine and a ballpoint pen rolled towards where she'd put the papers. She picked it up to hand it to me; her hand shook, and she dropped the pen. It rolled and fell to the floor. I reached down for it but she was closer and snatched it up. She stepped away and showed me the engraving on the barrel. I squinted to read the faded gold script: *Runner-up, Single Sculls, 2009.*

'This is Colin's pen,' she said. 'How the hell did it get here?'

10

I thought about lying, telling her Hawes must have left it when he was here with McLean, but her distress stopped me. She slumped down onto the seat and looked up at me with troubled eyes.

'I knew he was going to do something,' she said. 'He's talked to you, hasn't he?'

She was pale and the hand holding the pen was shaking.

I nodded. 'You'd better have some coffee.' I poured some into a mug and put it in the microwave. When I took it out I held up the whisky bottle. She nodded and I added a solid slug. She put the pen down gently on the bench, wrapped both hands around the mug and took a sip.

'He was here,' I said. 'In fact he stayed the night. He told me a few things and left me a note.'

I had the note in my wallet. I fetched it from my jacket, unfolded it and gave it to her.

'Oh, Jesus,' she said. 'They'll . . .'

'Drink your coffee. Who'll do what?'

She shook her head and had a drink. 'I need to think.'

My coffee was cold. I heated it up and spiked it. I sat down opposite her. I didn't say anything. It gave me a chance to examine her more closely. At a guess she was in her late twenties; she had good skin and features, a combination that somehow didn't make her either pretty or plain. I remembered her pause before referring to Hawes on the phone and from her behaviour now it wasn't hard to guess at their relationship. Big, homely, freckled Hawes and stocky little Cathy. Good pair.

She drank the coffee and collected herself. When she looked at me her face was flushed, either from embarrassment or the whisky or both. 'He spoke about you,' she said. 'He said you were a smartarse but there was something else about you he liked.'

'I can live with that. I found him impressive in a quiet way.'

'Yes, Colin's quiet. That's one of the things I love about him. I suppose you've guessed about us.'

'Hard not to.'

'Mmm. We met at the Academy and were friendly. Then we were posted to different places and didn't meet again until the GCU was being . . . reconfigured.'

'A new lot of detectives, uniforms and civilians.'

'Did Colin tell you that?'

'Might have. Are we in an information exchange here, Constable?'

She visibly tightened up. 'What do you mean?'

'I'm working on a case that keeps crossing lines with the GCU. You can see from Hawes's note that he knows of a connection. I need to know more about the ... let's say outfall, from that unit.'

'Like what?'

'Like names.'

She laughed. 'No way.'

I shrugged. 'I won't be leaving it alone.'

'You probably should.'

'I can't.'

She put Hawes's pen in her bag, pulled out another one and had me sign two documents to do with the return of my gun. The .38 and the ammunition were in two separate plastic bags in her briefcase. She put them on the bench.

'I shouldn't be telling you this, but getting a weapon back isn't usually as easy as this. I think you may be in serious trouble. I can't say any more until I find Colin.'

'Maybe I could help.'

'I don't think so.'

'Look, Colin's told you things. I don't know how much. He's exposed now, I reckon, but perhaps you're not—or not as much. What about the Police Integrity Commission? Could you go to them?'

'With what?'

'Your concerns.'

'I'm a constable. My concerns, as you put it, are about much higher-ups.'

'Like who?'

'Nice try. Thanks for the coffee and the grog, Mr Hardy.'

'Cliff.'

'Cliff, then. My advice to you is to be careful and do something else. Serve some subpoenas, catch some welfare cheats.'

Her scorn set my mind racing. Kate Greenhall suspected her brother was murdered for some reason; Timothy Greenhall had dodgy police contacts and Colin Hawes hadn't used the words Precision Instruments for no reason.

'If your colleagues are somehow involved in the death of my client's son—have murdered my client's son, possibly—I'm going to find out who and do something about it.'

'Good luck and goodnight.'

She scooped up her papers, stuffed them in her briefcase and was halfway to the front door before I could move. I sat where I was and listened to the door slam. I followed her and checked the deadlock on the door and set the alarm. Then I did the same with the back door. The windows were barred, as most windows in Glebe are.

I spilled the bullets from the plastic bag and loaded the .38. I grabbed the shoulder holster from a drawer in the kitchen, slipped the gun into it, took it upstairs and hung it on one of the hooks on the back of the bedroom door. I rewrapped the spare bullets in their plastic bag, put them in a pocket of my leather jacket and hung that on another hook. I'd never put a gun under my pillow and wasn't about to start now, but there was no harm in taking a few precautions.

I knew I had to talk to Greenhall and that it'd be a very tricky interview. I wanted to talk to Frank Parker first but when I rang in the morning Hilde told me he'd gone to a two-day voluntary euthanasia workshop in Bowral. That alarmed me.

'What's wrong with him?'

'What's wrong with him is what's wrong with us all, Cliff, including you. He's getting older and he just wants to be prepared. You should think about it.'

'Not yet. What about you?'

She laughed. 'I'm twelve years younger than Frank and both my parents lived into their nineties. I'll tell him you called when he gets back. You could ring him on his mobile but I wouldn't advise it.'

'Why's that?'

'He's serious about this. He's done a lot of reading on it and he's going to ask a lot of questions and want real answers. He doesn't need any distractions. You know what he's like.'

'Yeah. Are you sure he's not . . .'

'Keeping something from me? No, I'm not, but I trust him, Cliff.'

I finished the call and sat thinking about trust for a few minutes. I couldn't have said that it was an outstanding feature of the relationships I'd had. Maybe I'd never deserved it. I decided to visit Megan and the boys. It was school holiday time and Ben would be at home with his hard question. I'd find trust there.

Thinking I might go to the gym after visiting Megan I drove to Newtown rather than walk and began the tedious process of looking for a parking space reasonably close to her place. As usual, the area was parked solid; even a bikie looking for a spot was having trouble. Eventually a car pulled out of one of the bays in Federation Street west of Camperdown Park and I slid into it. I was locking the car when I heard a roar of motorcycle exhausts and within seconds I was hemmed in by six or seven bikies, all but one of whom wore the Bravados insignia—the head of a Texas longhorn bull with glaring red eyes. One didn't—the Harley rider who'd tracked me there and pretended to be looking for a parking space.

A clutch of big, mostly young, hairy men sitting astride their ticking machines is a scary thing, especially in a quiet, dead-end street. Three of the riders had pillion passengers. The cleanskin held up his mobile phone and grinned at me with gap-toothed satisfaction.

'Teamwork,' he said.

'Congratulations,' I said. 'Nice bikes.'

He nodded to one of the biggest of his comrades who pulled a flexible leather cosh from his saddlebag. Those things are lead-weighted, and they hurt. 'You're coming with us, Hardy. Will it be the soft way or the fuckin' hard way?'

I was buying time for no good reason. 'Depends on where we're going.'

The spokesman gestured to another man, who took a black hood from his pocket. 'That's something you don't need to know. Now hand over the fuckin' keys, and get in the back.'

Three pillion passengers dismounted. This was obviously a planned operation and I had no plan at all. I decided not to risk the cosh. After boxing and some of the bashings I've endured I only have so many brain cells left.

I tossed the keys at the spokesman and he dropped the catch.

'Fuck you,' he said.

'You too,' I said. 'What you have to do is unlock the driver's-side door and reach in to unlock the back doors. Want me to show you how? You're a bit young to know these things.'

He wasn't provoked. He handed the keys to one of the non-riders to open the car. I got in the back and had a Bravado, smelling of tobacco and sweat, on either side of me. I let one of them drop the hood over my head. After that it was a matter of sound rather than sight—the engine starting, the backing out, and we were on our way. If they'd wanted to kill or harm me they could have done it on the spot. Evidently they had something else in mind, at least for now.

You read that people are able to sense the direction of travel when blindfolded and work out places and distances from the traffic noise, the turns, the ups and downs and such things. I couldn't. All I had was a sense of time. It was hot under the hood.

After what felt like an hour and just to annoy them I said, 'I'm going to need a piss soon. Prostate trouble.'

'Cook it,' the one on my left said.

'Runs well, doesn't it, the Falcon? And your bloke handles a manual pretty well, too. That's unusual these days for anyone under forty. Rides the clutch a bit though.'

The one on the right dug an elbow hard into my ribs. 'Shut the fuck up!'

I turned towards him. 'Listen, shithead, someone evidently smarter than you wants me for some reason and I'm more likely to oblige him if I'm without bruises and in a good mood.'

'I told you . . .'

'Let him talk,' the driver said. 'Means he's scared.'

'You'll be scared if I ever get you one on one.'

The driver didn't respond, underlining his point, which wasn't altogether wrong.

*

Traffic noise died away. The car stopped and they bundled me out. Both my arms were gripped and they steered me along a rough track and didn't mind when I stumbled. They laughed when I swore. The driver was evidently leading the way; smoke from his joint drifted back towards me.

'I need a piss,' I said.

I felt a shove in my back, lurched forward, put my hands out instinctively and felt the trunk of a tree.

'Make it quick,' one of them said and I did.

We got moving again and I felt grass and then concrete underfoot. A door opened and I was propelled over a step and into a space that smelled of cigarette smoke, beer and dog. My feet were kicked out from under me and I collapsed into an armchair that creaked but held.

'Get the hood off,' a voice said.

It wasn't the first time I'd been blindfolded and I knew better than to open my eyes at once. I lowered my head and opened them slowly, blinking carefully.

'This bloke knows what he's doing,' the voice said. 'He give you any trouble?'

'Only with his fuckin' mouth.'

I lifted my head and took in the scene. I was in the living room of what was probably a farmhouse to judge by the tongue-and-groove construction of the walls. There was a threadbare carpet, a fireplace and two windows, one of which was cracked and mended with sealing tape. Three men, all uniformed Bravados, all unfriendly.

The smallest of them, sitting in a chair opposite me, was the one who'd given the order to take off the hood. He was medium-sized and wiry with bushy ginger hair drawn back in a ponytail. Hard to guess his age; maybe thirty. He was clean-shaven with long sideburns and had clear pale skin as if he'd never been out in the sun. He wore blue-tinted granny glasses. One of the others, whose voice identified him as the driver, was taller, younger and very dark, so that it was hard to tell whether he had just fashionable stubble or a beard; the other was fairer and best described in one word—fat.

'I'm Paul,' the redhead said. He jerked his thumb at the others, dark and fat in turn. 'That's Bruce and Ray.'

'Paul who?'

'Just Paul. Now you'll agree that you haven't been hurt, just a bit ... inconvenienced. Right?' He had an educated voice that seemed to have been deliberately roughened.

'Bruce rode the clutch in my car. I could be up for a new one.'

Paul almost laughed but not quite.

'That's what he's like,' Bruce said. 'A smartarse. He needs a good kicking.'

I looked at him. 'I've told you, mate. I'll take you on any time.'

'This is all bullshit,' Paul said. 'What you're going to do is help us find who killed our brother Dusty Miller in Katoomba.'

'What would I know about that?'

'You were there.'

'Suppose I was, why would I help you?'

Paul leaned forward so that I got the full strength of his clove-scented breath. 'Because if you don't, you're going to join Dusty.'

11

There was no mystery to how they knew I'd been at Miller's place. Paul told me Miller had concealed miniature CCTV cameras installed inside and outside. Cameras as a defence against rival bikies and not discovered by the police.

'How come they didn't pick up the killers?'

'They did. Three guys in balaclavas. They tortured Dusty and then beat him to death. The cops don't give a shit,' Paul said. 'The only good bikie is a dead bikie.'

'A lot of people feel like that,' I said.

'How about you?'

I shrugged. 'People like dressing up. I had fun on a Honda when I was younger. Live and let live. I'm a libertarian when it comes to drugs so I don't care what you do there.'

'How about guns?'

'I worry about the collateral damage.'

'So do we. We try to minimise it. We're getting off the point here. You . . .'

'Don't you want to know why I was in Katoomba?'

Paul laughed. 'We know why you were there. The cops confiscated your fucking gun and you wanted a back-up.'

'Jesus,' I said, 'that's right about my gun but way off base about me wanting to buy one. I wanted to see Miller about something quite different. How did you know the police had taken my gun?'

'Just a guess. I know a bit about you, Hardy. Happened to you once before, didn't it?'

'Twice, in fact.'

Bruce, who'd been smoking another joint and shifting from foot to foot, finally lost patience. 'Fuck, Paul, who cares? Is the cunt going to be of any use or not?'

Paul was distracted, surprised at his authority being challenged, and Bruce was well on the way to being stoned. Continued passivity wasn't an option in this situation. I'd been preparing myself, slowly moving my feet to get a good purchase on the ratty carpet and marking exactly where Bruce was by the sound of his voice rather than looking. I came out of the chair balanced and moving fast. Bruce was taking a big toke and was unprepared for the right jolt I gave him well below the belt. He yelped, dropped the joint and instinctively covered his groin as he bent over. I lifted a knee hard under his jaw and felt the bones click and his teeth clash together. He went down spitting blood.

'That's enough, Hardy!'

Quick as a cat, Paul was on his feet and had a pistol

jabbed hard into my right ear. Very hard; I felt the skin split. I opened my hands in submission.

'I warned him,' I said.

'Big deal. He'll be more careful next time, if there is a next time for you. Sit the fuck down, Hardy. Ray, get us a couple of beers and clean that bugger up.'

I subsided into the chair as Ray got busy. Paul kept the pistol well beyond my reach but with his arm loose and nothing to stop him bringing it up to where it'd do some good. He sucked noisily and winced.

I pointed to my mouth. 'Got a bad tooth, Paul?'

'Yeah,' he said, 'and a temper to match. Let's stop pissing around. You know things and we know things and it makes good sense for us to work together.'

Ray hauled Bruce away and came back after a few minutes with a six-pack of VB cans. He tossed a can to me and one to Paul, who gestured for him to leave the rest.

'Piss off, Ray, and look after Bruce. Get Hardy's keys off him and bring them in here. If Bruce acts up you know what to do.'

I opened the can and took a drink. 'What should he do?'

'Bruce is an epileptic. What you did to him might set him off. He might need his medication and holding down.'

'If I'd known that I'd have tackled Ray.'

Paul swallowed a good half of his beer in two gulps and sucked at his bad tooth. 'Water under the bridge. Let's get down to business.'

'I don't know who killed Miller.'

'Have a guess as if your life depended on it.'

I sipped the beer and thought about it. I didn't think my life was at serious or immediate risk. This was no mindless petrol-head hooked on speed and violence. Without having the faintest idea of what it might be, I sensed that he had another agenda. I watched as he finished his can and registered with surprise that his fingernails were clean, relatively. I wondered if his comrades had noticed.

'Glad to see you're thinking hard,' Paul said. 'Take your time.'

He fumbled in a pocket of his sleeveless denim jacket, fished out two pills and swallowed them dry.

'Tooth bothering you?' I said.

'Yeah. Would you believe I'm scared of dentists? Struck some butchers when I was young.'

'It's painless these days. Greatest achievement of the twentieth century, along with being able to pause live TV.'

He snorted. 'You can't fuckin' snake-charm me, Hardy. What's it to be?'

I decided. I finished the beer and set the can down on the floor. 'I'm reaching for my wallet, okay?'

He nodded, but he kept control of the pistol as he had throughout our exchange. I took Hawes's note from my wallet, smoothed it out and handed it to him.

'What's this?'

I sketched matters in for him, with not too much detail and no names, enough to let him see that the police GCU was a player in a game that involved the corruption of officials and businessmen and almost certainly politicians as well. Canny man that he was, he listened without interrupting. When I'd finished he tapped the note.

'Who wrote this?'

'A cop, part of the GCU but not happy.'

'Name?'

I waggled my head from side to side and took another can from the pack. 'Have to be some mutual guarantees here, Paul. Some safeguards.'

'Against what?'

'Well, say, against the suspicion that someone in my position might have that you killed Dusty to get control of his gun stash.'

That got me my first real surprised reaction from him. 'Shit, Hardy,' he said, 'talk about a conspiracy theory.'

'Sometimes they're on the money.'

He moved his head to get a better look at the half-open door and tilted it as if listening for any movement from beyond it. Then he dropped his voice.

'You're way off beam. I'm not interested in Dusty's gun business. I don't know where he kept his guns. No one did.'

'Wasn't it covered by the CCTV?'

'No, Dusty was a super-suspicious bastard.'

'I thought you blokes were more fraternal than that.'

Still speaking quietly, he said, 'Oh, he shared the money out all right. Had to. So forget that idea. I've got other plans. Have another guess.'

'It looks as if there's a rogue element. A sort of offshoot, if you'll excuse the expression, from this police unit. They're not so much interested in combating gun crime as controlling it for their own ends.'

'Again, I'd like to hear some bloody names.'

I shrugged. 'No idea who the big fish are. The only two I know are very low level, the lowest, and not part of the deal. I'm not going to talk about them until we reach an understanding. I don't know how to contact them anyway, and they might not even know who's who. It might only be one or two ex-cops doing the dirty work with others covering for them.'

'That sounds like guesswork.'

'That's what you asked for.'

'Christ, you're a slippery bastard.'

'So are you. What's your game? You've got something going. If it's not to do with guns, what is it?'

He opened another can and took a drink. 'Pills've kicked in, thank Christ. All right, I'll tell you this much. I . . .'

'Easy,' I said. 'Sure the room's not bugged?'

For a split second, with his pain easing, he reacted, his eyes flicking around the shabby room before he recovered.

'Fuck you. Dusty was more than just a brother—he was the boss. Now I'm trying to be chief of the Bravados because I've got some plans. Long-term. I'm okay for now but I'll be rock solid if I can nail whoever killed Dusty. So I'll guarantee your personal safety and the safety of anyone you say is okay if you help me with that.'

'And how can you help me?'

'Point us in the right direction. We can watch people, follow them, frighten them.'

'Maybe, but you can't go around killing cops or even ex-cops.'

'Accidents happen.'

It was my time for meeting hard men to read, like Greenhall, like this one. Against all outward signs I had an impulse to trust him—at least to see where doing that took me.

'So they do. You'd better keep that in mind yourself. How do we stay in touch?'

'We've got this lawyer in Sydney—through him. Here's his card.'

'Where are we now, Paul?'

He grinned. 'Penrith, but it's not somewhere I'll necessarily ever be again.'

'Won't it look like weakness if you let me go?'

'It would but that's not what's going to happen.' He gestured with the pistol. 'Finish your beer and come outside.'

There was too much in the can for me to finish it quickly so I kept it in my hand as I left the room. Outside, a group of Bravados was gathered around the edges of a patch of scruffy grass about the size of a boxing ring. One of them bore a close resemblance to Bruce but was shorter and wider. Paul pointed to him.

'This is Terry. He's Bruce's brother and he reckons he's got a score to settle.'

Paul snapped his fingers and Ray tossed him my car keys. Paul lobbed them so that they fell at Terry's feet. 'There's your way out if you can get 'em.'

'You're a romantic,' I said.

Paul shrugged. 'And you're a wanker.'

His voice had resumed the roughness that had fallen away when he'd been talking to me privately. The man was an actor.

Terry said, 'You took Brucie by surprise.'

'That's right,' I said. I threw the can hard at his head, closed the gap between us in two steps and kicked him solidly in the crotch. He screamed; I pivoted and slammed my right elbow into the side of his head. He went down as if he'd been hamstrung. I scooped up my keys, walked to the Falcon and reversed it fast down the track with my hand hard on the horn as a parting insult.

12

They could easily have jumped on their bikes and come after me but they didn't. I spun around at the end of the track, took the first turn I came to and the next two until I found myself on tarmac. I fought the urge to speed and slowed down through the suburban streets. A few more turns and I was signposted to Penrith's CBD.

I drove slowly, enjoying what felt like the comradeship of the traffic, until I spotted a pub. Parking spaces galore. I pulled in and took a deep breath. The light was fading as the sun slipped down towards the mountain barrier from where the sunlit plains extended. I realised I was mentally babbling with relief. What if Paul hadn't retrieved and positioned the keys? What if Terry had got the better of me? What kind of arrangement had I entered into?

I went into the pub, got a double scotch and ordered a steak sandwich. I needed the comfort of the alcohol and the blotting effect of the food. Then coffee, plenty of coffee. Looking back, I had to admire Paul. He'd orchestrated things perfectly, put me under pressure but not to an extreme point. I'd kept my wallet and my mobile phone and he'd arranged for me to get to my car if I was up to it. He said he knew a few things about me; maybe he knew that someone who'd boxed, soldiered and survived in my profession for so long could handle a couple of angry, unprepared bikies.

I'd turned my mobile off when I'd left home. Now I turned it on and saw there were a couple of calls and texts. Megan had called asking when I was likely to visit. I rang and told her I'd try to visit in the morning. Viv Garner wanted to know if I'd got my gun back. I left the message that I had. One text was from Frank Parker. Hilde had evidently told him I'd called. All he said was that a shake-up was in progress and to keep my distance.

The other was from Cathy Carter, asking me to ring her urgently. I speared and ate a last chip and looked thoughtfully at my empty glass before pushing it aside and calling her number.

Her voice, previously low-pitched, was several notches higher. 'Mr Hardy, we need your help.'

'Who's we?'

'Colin and me. He's been assaulted . . . bashed.'

'How badly?'

'Not sure. I'm at Casualty at RPA. He's having tests.'

'Are the police involved?'

'Think what you're saying. I'm using a throwaway phone. I hope yours is secure.'

'Who knows? Stay there. I'm in Penrith. It'll take me a while to get to you. What've you told the staff there?'

'That he fell. It's true, as far as it goes.'

'Is either of you in uniform?'

'No. They're incredibly busy here. There's been some kind of street brawl in Camperdown.'

'Good. Stick close to other people. I'll get there as soon as I can.'

Casualty at RPA was buzzing with doctors and nurses rushing around while people waited to be seen, some bandaged, some with heads drooping towards their laps and nodding off from fatigue or drugs or alcohol, or all three. Cathy Carter, in jeans and a rugby shirt, was hunched over her iPad. She was at the end of a row of seats and I squatted down next to her.

'Hello, Cathy, have you heard any more?'

She nearly fell out of the chair and the tablet would have fallen if I hadn't caught it. She reached for me and our heads almost bumped.

'Fractured skull with pressure problems. They're going to operate. They're amazed that he was upright when I got him here. He collapsed during the examination.'

The woman sitting next to her moved away to give me her chair. I nodded my thanks and sat, putting my arm around Cathy's shoulders.

'Take it easy. A bloke like him'll come though it okay. What happened?'

'He was bashed. He said two of them, in balaclavas, broke into my place. I wasn't there. They bashed him with . . .'

'Batons?'

'No, those bloody great torches that weigh a ton. He said they only got in one good hit before he fought them off. He says he nearly crippled one of them and was about to deal with the other one but then he fell. The one he hurt was bleeding and moaning and the other one took him away. When I got back Colin was bleeding himself from a bad cut.' She touched the top of her head. 'He said he was all right but his eyes went funny and I drove him here. Jesus, those bastards!'

It wasn't the time to ask her how much she knew about what Hawes had been doing to bring this on. We waited and waited the way you do in Casualty. You can go up to the window and ask for more information as much as you like but they'll tell you only what they want to when they decide they can, and you've got no comeback.

The crowd thinned but others trickled in, now the people of the night—male and female, the very old and the very young. The weird thing was that, whatever the disparity between them in terms of sex and age, there was a sameness. They were damaged and the ones that brought them in sometimes looked only a little less damaged themselves.

I bought coffee from the machine twice and we drank it, although it tasted more of the plastic it came in than of coffee. Cathy started to wilt and she slumped against me, apologising for her weakness.

'Don't be silly,' I said. 'You've saved the man's life.'

'So I've saved my husband's life,' she murmured. 'That's what a wife's supposed to do, isn't it?'

'Husband?'

'We're married and you're the only other person in the whole fucking wide world that knows, Cliff Hardy.'

'I'm honoured.'

'You're honoured,' she said. 'What are you, a fucking knight of the round table?'

'Exactly,' I said.

She laughed. A doctor in scrubs and an anxious-looking nurse approached us.

'Ms Carter,' the nurse said. 'This is Doctor Selim Bashir.'

'I've operated on Mr Hawes,' the doctor said, 'and he's been put in an induced coma. I'm afraid we just have to wait and see how he responds from this point on.'

I took Cathy back to my place and went very carefully through my security procedures. She almost smiled when she saw me load the .38 and leave it where I could grab it quickly as I checked everything twice.

I showed her the spare room that Hawes had slept in a couple of nights back. I gave her a towel and a T-shirt and she reached up and kissed me on a cheek that would have been like a wire brush. I took the .38 with me and stretched out on the bed, shoeless but otherwise fully clothed. After the long and eventful day I was tired but my head was buzzing with the developing problems and dangers and I couldn't sleep until the beginnings of the early morning traffic noise lulled me off for a few hours.

Cathy slept late. I rang Megan and told her I couldn't get there that morning because something had come up.

'Very informative,' she said. 'Something hard?'

'Hard enough, as the actress . . .'

'Don't. Any way Hank or I can help?'

'Can you hack into a very, very secure police data repository?'

'Of course not. Why are you so often at odds with the cops, Cliff? Aren't you supposed to be on the same side?'

'I wish I knew,' I said. 'The force seems to have nourished some rough players.'

'What's it all about?'

I was upfront with Megan on a lot of things but not on this, not with guns and bashings in the mix. 'Money,' I said. 'Tell Ben I'm reading up on dinosaurs.'

'I have to warn you, he's taking an interest in aeronautics now.'

I heard Cathy showering as I made coffee. She came down looking fresh, the way small, blonde women with short hair can. My four-burner toaster only works on two slots. I busied myself preparing four slices of toast and heating a small jug of milk in the microwave and judging when to lower the coffee plunger. Cathy sat and watched me.

'Domesticated, aren't you?'

She was all set to take out her worries and frustrations on me. Some people are like that, but I wasn't going to let it happen.

'Yeah,' I said, 'so domesticated I spent most of yesterday being kidnapped by a pack of bikies because I suspect some of your colleagues, or ex-colleagues, had offed their leader with extreme prejudice. It was all about guns.'

She said nothing while I finished what I was doing and just nodded when I offered her coffee. We sat drinking hot flat whites and eating toast for a few minutes, thinking our own thoughts.

'I'm sorry,' she said. 'I didn't mean to sound so shitty. You've been very good. Can I use your phone to call the hospital?'

I nodded. She went to the phone in the living room and came back quickly.

'No change.'

'There was no media around when you went in, was there?'

'No, or if there was it was concentrated on the brawl victims. It was low-key for us at first and then everything went pear-shaped in the examining room. You think he's still in danger from . . . whoever?'

'I don't know, but I've got a rich client who could afford a guard if it became necessary.'

She pushed her mug and plate away. 'You'd better explain that. And what's this about bikies?'

'It was on the news—Dusty Miller, the Bravado boss, killed in Katoomba.'

She closed her eyes. 'Jesus,' she said. 'It fits.'

She explained that the GCU was originally divided into geographically based areas of command—northern beaches, western suburbs and Blue Mountains, city and eastern suburbs, and south.

'Colin survived the big 2013 bust-up in the unit because there was nothing against him and he was so good at the proper job. He thought things would be better but he became concerned about . . . other stuff.'

'I know a bit about this, Cath,' I said. 'From what he told me.'

'Okay. He was very stressed when we . . . got together. He had to talk to someone and he told me things about the cover-up of what the unit had done before.'

'And?'

'Particularly bad stuff in the Blue Mountains.'

I had to be careful. I didn't know how much Hawes had told her. Obviously something, but what?

'What stuff?'

'I don't know. He wouldn't say.'

'Bad stuff previously or still going on?'

Her glance was angry. 'Do you think I'm stupid? I know there's something bloody awful going on. I just don't know what. Colin wouldn't tell me. He just said the western division officers had been the real cowboys.'

'He talked a bit wildly,' I said. 'I wasn't sure how to take what he said. I liked him well enough, but he was . . .'

'Just a uniform. I know how contemptuous people like you are about us.'

She was getting wound up again and I was determined not to react.

'What sort of people do you mean, Cathy?'

'You were an officer in the army, weren't you? There's a photo of you up in that room with a woman I take to be your mother. You're all dolled up as a lieutenant and she looks that proud. And you're a friend of Frank Parker. Well, Colin was a wonderful, honourable man and he . . .'

'He's not dead, Cathy.'

She stopped in mid-sentence. 'Oh, God, this is a bloody nightmare.'

'All I meant was, how could he acquire all this intelligence from the position he held in the operation?'

'I don't know.'

'I hope you and Colin took precautions when you talked about this.'

'Of course we did. Some of our colleagues sussed what was going on between us and when we kept ourselves to ourselves more than normally they thought it was just that. Sex. Colin didn't want to tell me anything but you can't maintain a relationship like that, can you?'

'No, you're right. He didn't mention your name but he said there was someone else. I got the feeling it was someone he needed to protect. I thought he was going into hiding when he took off from here. Why would he go to your place when people knew about you two and he'd obviously put himself in someone's firing line?'

'I don't know.'

'He must've put something there he needed. Or something that would endanger you. Any idea what?'

Although it was early she was already close to emotional exhaustion from all the permutations. She shrugged. 'Christ knows.'

'We're going to have to find out,' I said. 'Because I doubt Christ is going to tell us.'

13

Cathy said she'd had a cryptic text message from Hawes, probably while he was still at my place.

'I couldn't contact him all day yesterday,' she said. 'So I called in sick this morning. I went to the doctor's to get a certificate, and when I got home I found Colin . . . the way he was.'

I reminded her about Hawes's note and told her about the Greenhall case and how it had involved me with cops, Hawes and now her. She asked to see the note again and read it several times, almost reverently.

'He trusted you,' she said. 'That wasn't easy for him to do with all this shit going on. I'll trust you, too.'

'Good. Now we have to assume Colin was spotted somewhere and followed to your place and that's where they attacked him, right?'

She nodded.

'We'll assume they thought he went there for comfort and not because he'd put something vital there. I'm guessing he meant to pick up whatever it was and go quickly, maybe leaving you some kind of message.'

'So maybe they think they've given him the signal to pull his head in. They don't know what he's got and they don't know how much he'd told you.'

'Have to hope that's right and that they're not after you.'

'I don't think they would be. Cops're chauvinistic bastards. A short-arsed chick with small tits and thick ankles wouldn't rank with them much.'

This was encouraging; she was toughening up by the minute.

'So it's somewhere between possibly and probably safe for us to search your place for whatever Colin hid there.'

'Between possible and probable's close enough for me. Have we got any allies, Cliff?'

It was a good question. 'There's Frank Parker, who you seem to know about. I don't know quite how he could help. He did say there was a shake-up in the force coming but that's all he said. I'm going to have to talk to Timothy Greenhall; he's the rich client I mentioned. I need to know more about him but you saw the note—Colin implies he's involved with the GCU. Greenhall needs to be told that this might have something to do with his son's death. There must be more he could tell us. And then there's this guy.'

I took the card Paul had given me from my wallet and held it so we could both look at it. The card was heavy duty and elegantly embossed. It announced Arthur Soames-Wetherell, SC, and gave his address as Pennyfeather Chambers in Martin Place, with fax and phone numbers and an email address.

'Soames-Wetherell,' Cathy said in a plummy accent. 'Pennyfeather . . . and this is a bikie's brief?'

'He's no ordinary bikie,' I said.

Cathy's flat was in Stanmore, close to the station. It was in a small block of four, plain looking from the outside but solid, worth a bit and appreciating because of its position, and I wondered if she owned it.

'You're wondering if I own it,' she said as we pulled up outside in a taxi. Both our cars were well known by the police and mine by the Bravados. We'd probably need replacements—another call on Greenhall's pockets.

'I wonder about everything,' I said.

'I do, thanks to my dead mum, okay?'

She was touchy and needed careful handling; stress was causing her to have mood swings, not the best thing in a partner, if that's what she'd become. We went up a narrow cement path past a scrap of lawn to a set of steps leading to a small porch.

'Front ground-floor flat,' Cathy said, 'no view, noisiest and cheapest until an airport noise program double-glazed us for free.'

She used a key to open the door into a short passage giving access to flats one and two. Another key opened her security screen and front door. Ordinary keys, a breeze for anyone half expert. I held her back, took the .38 from its holster and went cautiously in without the theatrics you see on the screen. If someone serious is waiting for you in a situation like that it doesn't matter how many hands you have on your gun; if you're not quick you're dead.

All clear. She pushed past me and pointed to the signs of Colin Hawes's struggle—a broken chair, displaced books, a broken vase and spots and streaks of blood on the rug.

'Did they teach you search technique at the Academy?'

'Yes and I was good, found every bloody thing they'd hidden. I'll take the bedroom and you start here. Apart from that and the kitchen there's only the little room I use as an office and the bathroom and toilet.'

'What about the floor?'

'Plastic fake wood veneer over a slab.'

'Manhole?'

'In the small room. Bit obvious, wouldn't you think?'

I shrugged and started in on the living room. I worked the chairs and couch over, feeling the upholstery and probing the padding. Nothing. The two bookshelves were stacked with hardbacks and paperbacks ranging from psychology to chick lit. The dust told me they hadn't been disturbed for a while. I reflected that if Hawes had come here to recover something and there'd been time for him to be attacked, his hiding place must have been somewhere it'd take a while to get to.

There were three pictures on the walls—a Turner print, a moody framed black and white photograph of a beach somewhere and one of a Police Academy graduating class. Hawes, one of the tallest, was in the back row; Cathy, one of the shortest, was in the front. I took them down and investigated the backings with the result I expected. None.

After a bit more moving of ornaments and unscrewing of light fittings with no result, I stood in the middle of the room and tried to think. What would I do if I'd hidden something in my girlfriend's flat and came to retrieve it? If I thought I was safe for a while? First I'd probably have a drink. But nobody hides things in refrigerators anymore, if they ever did. Then what? It's the twenty-first century. *I'd think computer.*

I went into the small room that would catch the morning sun at the front of the flat. A big blank computer screen stared at me from a desk. There was barely room for the desk and the swivel chair; a lot of the space was taken up by a three-tiered shelf crammed with CDs and DVDs.

I went out to the kitchen, opened the fridge and took out a stubby of beer, popped the cap and took a drink while leaning against the clean-as-a-whistle sink. Cathy must have heard me moving around because she came into the room with her frustrated-and-it's-all-your-fault face on.

'What the hell are you doing?' she said.

'Cathy,' I said, 'how well d'you know your movies and music?'

It took quite a while with our excitement mounting, but the result was a big letdown. There was nothing out of place, nothing concealed. Cathy swore and looked at me. I swore too.

'I've been so dumb,' I said. 'He wouldn't hide anything here to expose you to danger.'

'Where then?'

'Where did he go seeking shelter from the storm?'

'Your place.'

We found the disks in a batch I kept in the spare room. Music I thought I'd like and didn't—a Guy Clark tribute album, a Ray Charles duet effort, some inferior Merle Haggard and a few others. The disks were in a case with something written on the spine in Italian. It wasn't Mario Lanza or even Pavarotti.

We went back up to the spare room, which doubles as my 'home office', and I booted up the computer.

Cathy inserted one of the disks and the message that came up required a password.

'Do you know his password?'

'Of course. You're obviously not married now, but were you once?'

'Yes.'

'And did you conceal things from your wife?'

'Yes.'

'I'm not surprised. Look away.'

She was in charge now and I did as she asked. She typed in the password.

'It's audio,' she said and hit the appropriate key.

'Is this a secure line, Chas?' a male voice said.

'No names, for Christ's sake.'

'So it's not secure?'

'It's fucking secure, don't worry about that, but I'm worried about you.'

'I told you at the time why I did it.'

'Yeah, yeah. But this next thing . . .'

'It's necessary.'

'I wonder. I fucking wonder.'

'He's ratshit. He'll talk under pressure. D'you want a meeting?'

'I hate fucking meetings.'

'Didn't always. You loved them, mate.'

Laughter.

'Kill it,' I said.

'Why? There's more.'

'I bet there is. Lots more. But this isn't the time or place to listen to it.'

She ejected the disk. 'Who was ratshit?'

'Who knows? Dusty Miller, probably, or someone we don't even know about.'

'Your client, for example?'

On the attack again, she was remorseless.

'That's our next port of call anyway. He's someone who might not want to talk to us. You and that disk could be useful.'

She put the disk back in the case and dropped it into the shoulder bag she carried and challenged me to object. I shrugged and drank the dregs of the beer I'd opened on the way in.

'Talk to people who don't want to talk. That's what you do, isn't it? Do you enjoy it?'

'Sometimes, usually after the event.'

'Mr Enigmatic,' she said. 'Where're we going?'

'Where the money is. We're going to need some.'

I phoned Greenhall's factory and finally got through to him after several attempts by minions to fend me off.

'You say it's important,' Greenhall said without preamble.

'It is.'

'What have you found out?'

'Too much and not enough. I have to see you and I mean now.'

'Now? I've got a hundred things . . .'

'Nothing as important as this, Tommy.'

'What did you call me?'

'I called you Tommy. Want the full moniker? How about Tommy Greenfall, pistol shooter?'

Silence at the end of the line, then, 'Okay, where and when?'

'My office as soon as you can make it.'

He had one last try. 'I don't like your tone.'

'I don't like using it. I'll be waiting.'

I cut the call and got ready to use the phone again. Cathy stopped me.

'I want to check the hospital.'

I handed her the phone and she rang the number. All she could say was things like 'Yes, I understand,' and 'Thank you'.

'No change,' she mumbled, handing me the phone. Then she pulled herself together and looped the strap of her bag over her shoulder. 'Do you always talk to your clients like that?'

'Clients in my game are like witnesses in yours,' I said. 'Sometimes friendly, sometimes hostile.'

'Deep,' she said.

She wasn't easy to get along with. I wondered how Hawes had managed in the past and how, and if, he would again.

14

Another taxi, another tense silence between us. I ushered her into the office. She looked sceptically at the spartan fittings.

'A one-man band,' she said.

'Absolutely.'

'Where's he going to sit?'

'Good point.'

There was a storeroom on this level where the various tenants kept things they didn't need or want in their offices. I went down the corridor to it, unlocked the door and fossicked for a chair of some kind. I pulled out a well-used folding number that would have to do. I carried it back to the office where it immediately became unnecessary because Constable-on-sick-leave Cathy Carter had gone.

They made a fine pair, Colin and Cathy, good at disappearing when it suited them. She couldn't go far while Hawes was in hospital and her staying with me suggested she didn't have any close friends, but maybe that was wrong and she just stuck because I was in the mix of what was happening. I tried to remember whether she'd reacted with recognition to the recorded voices or to the mention of 'Chas' but I couldn't recall.

I stood by the window looking down into the street and trying to guess which of the cars that appeared was likely to belong to Greenhall. After a few wrong choices I gave up. Eventually a black Audi that had circled the block cracked it for a parking space. Greenhall, wearing a suit but no tie, got out and crossed the street quickly. He had the same stiff I-can-cope walk as the last time I'd seen him.

Purposeful footsteps in executive leather on the stairs. I held the door open for him. He glanced at the fold-up chair leaning against a filing cabinet.

'Expecting someone else?'

'No, that was for you. Someone was sitting where you can sit now. She left unexpectedly.'

Uninterested, he nodded and sat. 'So you now know more about me than you did.'

I went back behind the desk, took out Hawes's note and slid it across to him. He hooked on a pair of rimless glasses and read it. 'Who wrote this?'

The only way to answer was to give him a summarised version of what had happened since I'd accepted his case. I held back some details for their possible shock value. I included the speculation that he didn't believe his son had suicided. He listened in silence but his nod confirmed that point.

He pointed to his chair. 'Was this for whoever wrote the note?'

'No, he's in hospital fighting for his life. Now you're going to tell me your real reason for hiring me or I'm going to drop the whole thing.'

'No you won't. You didn't mention Frank Parker by name but I know about you and him. You'll get his help, for sure, and your reputation is for persistence.'

Jesus, I thought. *Another one on about me and Frank.*

'Not necessarily on the first point,' I said. 'And I only persist when I feel I can trust my client at least halfway, so I still want some answers.'

Greenhall tucked his chin down towards his chest and I noticed for the first time that his hair was thinning on top. Like a lot of men in that condition he avoided letting people see the top of his head but his distress had lowered his guard. He sighed and, again a first for him, fidgeted in his chair. Actions can speak louder than words: I could see now that he was basically a very secretive man and it pained him to tell the whole truth.

'It begins back when I got my start. You obviously know about the pistol-tampering business. Well, I'm a strong character, I think, at least I was then. I put all that behind me. I changed my name, did the degree and I had ideas, great ideas.

'I needed start-up capital. I couldn't go for a loan because the other stuff was too fresh and any enquiry would be likely to turn it up. I knew a couple of cops from my shooting days and you didn't have to be a genius to know that they were bent and greedy. In my university holidays I'd worked for a number of big firms as a sort of intern, although we didn't use the word back then. I was doing economics as well as engineering and I was useful in lots of ways. I could see how these places could be robbed blind. Shit . . . I can't believe . . .'

He was sweating now. I slid the box of tissues across to him and he mopped his face.

'Go on,' I said.

'I'm not trying to make excuses for what I did, but these companies weren't squeaky clean themselves. They were hiding money and laundering it and their payroll protection arrangements were a joke. I helped the police stage two payroll robberies and one break-in that netted them a lot of money and then I helped the companies cover up the losses with . . . creative accounting. Things were a lot looser then—no ICAC, dodgy auditors, fat cats in the ATO who knew bugger-all about trusts and offshore accounts. You get the picture.'

I nodded. 'This is Nugan Hand Bank days.'

'A bit later, quite a bit, but same sort of thing. Anyway, I got a . . . commission from various sources and that's how I got my start. I should've said that I modified some of the pistols for the hold-up guys—removed serial numbers and changed them so they could never be traced to anyone if they should turn up. One did get used and was dumped by a rogue cop, and the examination into it led nowhere.'

'All that exposed you to some pretty dangerous people.'

'I know, so I took out insurance.'

'Insurance?'

'I have technical skills you wouldn't believe. I taped and filmed some of the meetings and discussions.'

'That was dangerous, too.'

'It was a long time ago and I was well ahead of the technological curve. The companies are mostly defunct, and some of the police involved are dead or retired.'

'But not all.'

He sighed. 'No, not all. That's where Patrick comes in. We never got on well. I was too busy, I think I told you that.'

'What about his mother?' I interrupted. 'Where was she in all this?'

He gave me a sharp look, as if wondering who I'd been talking to.

'She knew nothing about it. Jilly was very young when I married her. We had the children pretty quickly but ... motherhood didn't suit her. It was a mistake. She resented everything about me and Patrick reminded her of me. Kate wasn't ever Jilly's idea of a feminine creature even when she was young. It was all a mess.'

He shook his head, as if surprised at telling me so much.

'Then when Patrick got the museum job I tried to get on better terms with him and I let him look at some of my early designs and prototypes with a view to contributing them to the museum. And just as I'd done, he started looking into things. Snooping. I had my insurance safely hidden, so I thought, but Patrick came across it. We had a row. He threatened to expose me.'

'What did you do?'

'I got someone to break into his flat and collect the evidence—the films and tapes—he'd taken away. I destroyed it in front of him. Then he was killed. When I saw what had happened I knew that the people I'd dealt with back in the day had done it. It had their stamp.'

'Killed why?'

'Because he'd seen the films and heard the tapes.'

'How would they know that?'

'He must have told someone, one of his drug contacts perhaps. Who knows what an addict will say?'

'I thought he was clean by the time he had the museum job.'

Greenhall shook his head. 'He tried.'

'Better to kill you.'

'No, I'd told them I had copies and that I'd made preparations for them to go to the appropriate places if I was harmed. It wasn't true. I didn't have copies, but I've often found threats themselves have force, whether they can be backed up or not. Killing Patrick was a warning to me to continue as before.'

I sat back and tried to let all this sink in. Even if it was basically true there were gaps and questions. There was one in particular but I decided to hold back on it. I had my own agenda now. Greenhall was staring at nothing, seeing nothing.

'If I can sort any of this out it's going to cost you.'

'I know. It's already cost me my son.'

'Now we get to it, Mr Greenhall,' I said. 'You knew Patrick was murdered, so what was your real motive in coming to me?'

'I knew that once you started investigating something would shake loose. I knew Parker would help you. I thought it would lead to whoever murdered my son.'

'You're a very duplicitous man, Mr Greenhall.'

'You have no idea.'

'You must know the names.'

He shook his head. 'Four or five names only. I don't know which of them are alive or dead or how to contact them. If I'd told you all this at the start you'd have sent me on my way.'

'Probably,' I said. 'As it is, your plan to shake things loose has put a couple of admirable people who came to me for help in great danger and stretched my relationship with an old friend.'

'I'm sorry.'

'Are you? I doubt it. Just suppose I can find out who's responsible and Frank Parker can help to get a clear run at him or them. That'll expose you when all the dirty washing gets aired.'

'Mr Hardy, my wife is mentally unbalanced, my son's been murdered because of me and my daughter dislikes me although I've tried to help her financially. On the other hand,

I've produced some things that have benefited humanity and there's one more major advance in surgical equipment I have to see through some very complex financial, political and technological stages. Whatever happens now, however much dirty washing you air, I calculate there's time enough for me to get the project accepted. After that, I really don't care.'

15

I was sure Greenhall still hadn't told me everything. There was the question that Harry's student contact had raised about how Precision Instruments had stayed afloat. It hadn't seemed appropriate to bring it up while Greenhall had been in confessional mode, but it left me wondering whether he'd continued his association with criminals he'd helped from time to time early on. It was a definite possibility.

He left and I watched him walk to his Audi. He was upright and purposeful, very much the CEO. I remembered commenting in our first interview that his son had some heavy burdens. Well, Greenhall was carrying his share and hiring me hadn't exactly off-loaded them.

It was well after midday; I poured a glass of white wine and washed down the required pills. That left me feeling hungry. I walked to the delicatessen a few blocks away, bought a salad sandwich and took it back to the office.

I put the half-full wine glass on the desk along with the sandwich and the piece of paper on which Greenhall had written five names in his neat, slightly back-sloping script:

Owen Patmore
Charlie Henderson
Luke Soames
Tony Cantello
'Rooster' Fowler

Two of the names jumped out at me. 'Charlie' could be the 'Chas' in Hawes's recording and Soames-Wetherell was the name of bikie Paul's lawyer. Connections—the investigator's friend, sometimes the only friend. Good wine, good sandwich and a shaft of optimism to go with them.

I rang the hospital and was told that Hawes was showing signs of improvement but was still a long way short of normal function.

'Has he had any visitors?' I asked.

'Only his wife.'

'What are the visiting hours?'

'There aren't any in intensive care.'

No help. With the list of names, Cathy Carter might be able to identify the voices on the recording now but where was she? Not at home, that was for sure, but close by, almost certainly. But I didn't fancy hanging around RPA for who knew how long waiting for her to turn up. Efficient watching takes manpower.

I finished the wine and the sandwich and brushed the crumbs and the wrapper into the wastepaper bin. That just left the note and those names, especially Soames. I took the card Paul had given me from my wallet. I was frustrated and impatient but I told myself not to be. There was no urgency. What I needed was calm, efficient procedure, something I have never been very good at.

I rang Viv Garner and asked him what he knew about Arthur Soames-Wetherell SC.

'He's not the man for us,' Viv said, 'we don't need him.'

'Us? We?'

'I assume you've got yourself in the shit again and need a barrister. Not him.'

'Why not?'

'He's a comedian. Tells jokes to juries.'

'I like him already. Does he win?'

'Wins some, loses some.'

'Don't we all? No, I just have to talk to him about something and wanted to be sure he's not a bagman in somebody's pocket.'

'There you go again with the crummy jokes. You'll get along well with Arthur. No, he's okay. Eccentric, does pro bono work for asylum seekers, rides a bike to his chambers.'

'A motorbike?'

'No, a pushbike. Why did you say that?'

'Just a thought.'

'Your thought processes are weird.'

'I hope so.'

'Should I be standing by?'

'No, mate. I'm playing this by the book.'

'I'll stand by, then.'

I rang Pennyfeather Chambers, gave my name, and was put through promptly to Soames-Wetherell.

'Mr Hardy,' a light musical voice said, 'I've been expecting your call.'

The Pennyfeather Chambers housing Soames, Pearson and Soames-Wetherell were on level three of a building in Martin Place with a medical insurance office on the ground floor. That seemed appropriate because a quick web check of the legal firm revealed that it had a specialty in medical malfeasance. The lift took me up to a carpeted and well-appointed reception area with a well-appointed young woman behind the desk. She used the intercom and directed me down a passage to Soames-Wetherell's office. Some of the rooms I passed had glass doors and walls but Soames-Wetherell was ensconced behind solid oak. I knocked, got the call and went in.

The lawyer was already on his feet and moving towards me. Fifty plus, medium-sized, trimly built with greying auburn hair and a neat beard. The suit, the shirt, the tie, the shoes, the desk, the bookshelves, the conference corner were all standard fittings; the only offbeat note was the foldaway bicycle leaning against an ornate coat rack that held a helmet, gloves and a padded parka.

His handshake was firm. He steered me to the conference corner where there was a table with six chairs. He left the head-of-the-table chair vacant and sat down opposite me.

'Paul told me you'd be in touch,' he said.

'Paul is your . . .?'

'My nephew. My sister's boy.'

'And what did he tell you?'

He held up his hands. 'Whoa, now. That's not how it works, with all due respect. Paul's well disposed towards you, I must say. Admiring even, which is unusual for him. I need to know why you're here.'

'And I need to know what sort of person he is, because I want his help and I have to know if I can trust him.'

'To do what?'

'To play a part in a very tricky situation and not to let his interests override mine.'

He leaned back in his chair. 'That's a tall order. Paul's a hard man to dictate to.'

'First he was a boy, now he's a man. We have an interest in common, but unless I get some assurance that there's not going to be some bikie freak-out, I'll be on my way and you can tell him we had a pleasant chat.'

'You and he are very alike.'

'Not so's you'd notice.'

'I mean the direct assertiveness. It's a rare quality.' He

waved his hand in the air. 'Most people . . . lack all conviction, while . . .'

'Yeats,' I said. 'Don't patronise me, Mr Soames-Wetherell.'

'I'm sorry. You want to know about Paul. He's a remarkable man, extremely intelligent. He acquired two degrees by correspondence while . . .'

'Being a bikie.'

'While serving three years in the navy as a diver, three in the Timor peacekeeping force and, yes, as a bikie. He saved lives in Timor through his diving skills and again in his . . . present role.'

'How many convictions?'

Soames-Wetherell smiled. 'You're provoking me. None at all.'

'Not even with the present crackdown?'

'That's absurd and it'll pass. In fact I think there'll be a backlash against it. People imagine the motorcycle clubs are monolithic. They aren't. They're factionalised, and the Bravados are a prime example. True, there's a criminal element, focused on guns and drugs. I believe you saw one of the consequences of that.'

'Dusty Miller, yes. Very unpleasant.'

'Just so. There's another element that's devoted to the welfare of ex-service personnel suffering from post-traumatic-stress syndrome, substance abuse and various forms of social and mental disability. Paul heads that group and struggles every day to try to shift the focus of the Bravados and other clubs to those kinds of concerns.'

'I find that hard to believe.'

'Do you? It doesn't mean they don't make money from drugs and welfare and insurance fraud. He once pointed out to me that it was exactly what pharmaceutical companies and a sizeable number of the rest of the population do. You spent some time with them. Did Paul appear to have authority?'

'Up to a point.'

'Did he express any interest in taking over Miller's illegal enterprises?'

'No.'

'Did he contrive to speak with you in private?'

I nodded.

'How did he handle the more violent members of the club?'

I thought about it and his actions came vividly back to me. 'I'd say he manipulated them and me to achieve the result he wanted.'

He shrugged. 'There you are.'

'So he's clever and manipulative. Is he trying to achieve respectability for the Bravados and others?'

Soames-Wetherell smiled. 'I wouldn't go that far.'

'It's a pipe dream.'

'It probably is, but those people I've mentioned need some help and he'll supply it, as best he can, at least for a while. It's better than nothing. What're these spineless governments who throw young people into these hell holes as part of their geopolitical strategies doing for them when they come out covered in shit?'

I stared at him and he stared back. 'Not every SC in a smart suit is a right-winger, Mr Hardy. Because I can afford to, I do some pro bono legal work for the kinds of people Paul helps in practical ways. Or tries to, against the odds. I pose as an erratic eccentric, but I crack some nuts from time to time.'

I sat back and thought about what he'd said. This uncle and nephew were something else, something new to my experience. He left me to think while he went to a coffee machine in a recess and did things. After a few minutes he brought back two plastic cups of dark, aromatic coffee.

'No milk, I'm afraid. Don't believe in it. Nothing dairy or metal should touch coffee, ever.'

I'd heard that before. I sipped the coffee and, again, it tasted as good as it smelled. 'What's Paul's surname, by the way?'

He smiled. 'Soames or Wetherell, according to what suits him at the time. The name sort of drifts around in the family, sometimes with the hyphen, sometimes not. To pick up your point, it may be a pipe dream but it's Paul's dream, at least for now.'

'And when it snuffs out?'

'I believe he'll go into politics.'

I almost choked on the next sip of coffee. 'That's bizarre.'

'Is it any more bizarre than Godwin Grech fooling Malcolm Turnbull, James Packer at Barangaroo and Tony Abbott becoming prime minister?'

'I suppose not.'

'There's a call for MPs to have more experience than a law degree and a stint as a political staffer or a union official. Paul would meet that requirement well and truly. Now, what did you want him to do for you?'

'Watch out for someone, possibly follow them. Depending on how things develop, give me some back-up if things get sticky.'

'I see, and what would you do for him?'

'With luck, find out who killed Dusty Miller.'

'I hope you realise, Mr Hardy, that while you see this interview as you getting an assessment of Paul, he'll see it as him getting an assessment of you through me.'

'Hard to miss that.'

'To answer your basic question, I'd say Paul would be capable of handling what you want. And if you can identify who killed Miller he'd consider himself in your debt.'

'Would he exercise restraint if it came to that? Or, rather, would he be able to control his . . . criminal elements, as you call them?'

He spread his hands. 'Hard to say. More coffee?'

'No thanks. What assessment of me will you give him?'

'Positive, within limits.'

'What limits?'

He smiled. 'Still under consideration. While we're navel gazing, what did Viv Garner tell you about me?'

Inevitably, my attention drifted to the bike. 'He said we'd get along because we both tell crummy jokes.'

He laughed. 'Well we haven't done that, have we?'

'Got along?'

'No, told crummy jokes.'

'There's time left. If you . . . endorse me to Paul I'll need a way to contact him quickly.'

'You're trying to anticipate my decision.'

'That's right.'

'Nice try.'

The angle of the head and the tone of voice were precisely the same. 'You sound just like him.'

'We're close. I'll email you. I have your details from the website.'

I stood slowly, trying not to let joints crack and show how much I needed the stretch.

'One last thing, Mr Soames-Wetherell. Luke Soames, policeman, any connection?'

'A cousin.'

'Are you in touch?'

'I don't go to séances.'

'He's dead?'

'So we believe. He disappeared about . . . oh, about twenty years ago. Good afternoon, Mr Hardy.'

16

I'd walked from my office to the lawyer's chambers in the city and now I walked back again. A web search on the names Greenhall had given me turned up information only on Owen Patmore and Grantley 'Rooster' Fowler. Patmore had competed as a pistol shooter at Commonwealth and Olympic games and had retired as an inspector from the police service in 1993. He'd died of a heart attack three years later. I crossed him off the list.

Fowler was charged with perjury, falsifying evidence and conspiring to pervert the course of justice. He served three years in prison and was discharged from the police. I put a tick beside him and a question mark beside Luke Soames.

My inbox pinged and there was a message from Soames-Wetherell consisting of nothing more than a mobile phone number. I rang it.

Paul's smoother voice. 'Yes, Hardy?'

Well, I thought, *he said he had my number.*

'I've been to see your uncle Arthur.'

'Obviously, and . . .?'

'He seems to think we can work together on a you scratch my back and I'll scratch yours basis.'

'Who scratches first?'

'You do. I want you to watch visitors to the intensive care ward of the Royal Prince Alfred Hospital in Camperdown. Have you got someone who can hang around there and not chew tobacco and spit on the floor?'

An exasperated sigh came over the line. 'Go on.'

'There's a woman, thirtyish, short, blonde, medium build, who'll visit a man named Hawes. I want her followed and the address of where she's staying. She's a cop on leave and smart. I don't want her spooked.'

'And then?'

'I talk to her. And you become the beneficiary of whatever I learn.'

There was a snort of laughter. 'You spent too long with Uncle Arthur picking up the legal chat. That sounds all right. What about Greenhall?'

I was sure I hadn't mentioned Greenhall to him. 'Who?'

'I believe Uncle Arthur tried to high-hat you by quoting Yeats and you told him not to think you were dumb.'

'Something like that.'

'Same here. You showed me that note. How long do you think it took me to find a company called Precision Instruments and learn a bit about it?'

'You take the points.'

'Don't forget it.'

'We'll get to Greenhall in time.'

'When is this woman likely to visit?'

'I don't know; that's why I can't do the job myself.'

'Because you'll be busy doing what?'

'Investigating.'

The snort came again. 'I'll be in touch.'

'How's the tooth?'

'I took your advice. I went to the dentist and had it pulled. When something goes bad on me I get rid of it.'

I sat back and thought through the day's developments. I wasn't exactly stalled, I had balls in the air, but nothing was likely to happen imminently. Presumably it would take some time for Paul to set up his watcher and there was no telling when Cathy would visit Hawes. It depended on his condition and whatever, if anything, she had in mind to do. I planned to ring Frank Parker and ask him about the names on Greenhall's list, but I'd pushed Frank a bit too hard last time and thought it best to wait a while. I could do with a mental break.

I rang Megan.

'Fit us in, can you?' she said.

'Fair go, love. I . . .'

'Cliff, I was pulling your leg. Jesus, if you lose your sense of humour you're fucked.'

'I know. I've been told today that my crummy jokes were part of my appeal. I'll have to be careful.'

'We'd all love to see you.'

'How about sevenish?'

'I'll order in Lebanese.'

'I'll pay.'

'Don't overdo it.'

'Is Ben still into aeronautics?'

'Entomology.'

'Jiminy Cricket!'

She laughed. 'See you then.'

I drove to Newtown and cruised the streets around Megan's flat, not only to kill time but to be sure I didn't have a motorcycle escort or any other kind of tail. I tried to switch off from the case but little snippets kept jumping in at me. I realised I should have told Paul the kind of car Cathy drove to help his watcher. I smiled to myself as I thought how the conversation might have gone.

'Registration?'

'Didn't get it.'

'Call yourself a detective?'

The visit went well. Ben popped his question as soon as I was through the door.

'Cliff, how many legs does a centipede have?'

'Gidday, Benny, nice to see you, a hundred.'

'Wrong. It's forty-two. They just called it a centipede, like a hundred, because it was a lot.'

'And they'd be hard to count.'

'Yeah, except under a microscope. I wish I had a microscope.'

I looked enquiringly at Megan and Hank.

'For Christmas, maybe, if the interest lasts.'

I read Jack a couple of stories before bed. Ben was allowed to watch an episode of *The Night Garden* before he was packed off with his creepy-crawly encyclopedia.

We demolished the Lebanese meal, with Megan getting up from time to time to deal with the boys.

'How's it going, Hank?'

'Real well. Paranoia's good for business.'

Hank had learned the PIA business from me. Got qualified and set up on his own. These days he specialises in sweeping for listening devices, installing security systems and various IT functions beyond my understanding or wish to understand. He told me that the Romanian gang skimming ATMs and reaction to the UK phone hacking scandal had brought in work.

'Thank you, Rupert,' I said.

He raised his glass.

'What are we toasting?' Megan said when she returned.

'It's who,' I said. 'Rupert Murdoch.'

She scooped up some hummus onto a bit of flatbread. 'The Dirty Digger, eh?' she said. 'Screw him.'

17

I slept late the next day. I showered, I shaved. I made and ate a bigger breakfast than usual and listened to Radio National longer than usual. I was putting off phoning Frank Parker, but Cathy Carter saved me the trouble. When I was halfway up Glebe Point Road to buy the paper my mobile rang. It was Frank.

'Cliff, what the hell have you been up to?'

'Where d'you want me to start? What's happened?'

'I've just had a hysterical phone call from a woman claiming to be a police officer and saying she's involved with you in a police corruption investigation.'

I don't like talking while walking. I sat on a brick wall and swore because it was damp from overnight rain.

'What?' Frank said.

'It's nothing. That was Constable Cathy Carter, attached to the GCU. Her husband, who's also a GCU officer, is in hospital in intensive care. I'm investigating a murder, not police corruption, but I have to tell you the lines intersect.'

'Didn't I advise you to steer clear of the GCU?'

'Couldn't help it, Frank. It's not the unit itself, not directly, it's . . .'

'Not now. Is this woman in danger?'

'Yes.'

'Where is she?'

'I don't know, but I've taken steps to find her. I've . . .'

'I'm coming over to see you. You can give me all the bloody details then. I hope you haven't cocked things up by blundering in.'

'Cocked what up?' I said, but the line went dead.

Frank arrived an hour later looking angry and not his usual cool self. We've known each other longer than I care to remember and mostly rub along perfectly well with just the occasional hiccup. This felt more like a serious breach.

We nodded at each other as if neither knew what to say, until we were in the kitchen and I was making coffee. It was petty of me but I wasn't going to break the silence. Frank is retired and I'm still working and entitled to make some mistakes. Plus, I didn't think I had.

Frank accepted the coffee and stirred three spoonfuls of sugar into it. I'd never seen him do that before, although I know my coffee always turns out bitter.

'Who's in hospital?' he said at last.

'Acting Sergeant Colin Hawes.'

Frank sipped his coffee but clearly didn't even taste it. 'How does he come to be in hospital?'

'Piecing things together, it looks as though he was gathering evidence on GCU people's connections with ... rogue elements—sort of faces from the past. Seems to have stumbled onto some revealing stuff.'

'What stuff?'

'Recorded phone conversations.'

'Jesus. Who has that material?'

'Constable Carter has some. If there's more only Hawes knows where it is.'

'What put him in hospital?'

'Two men in balaclavas wielding those kinds of heavy torches used by ...'

'Okay, okay. Has he got any protection?'

'He was admitted by his wife as the victim of an accidental fall.'

'Is he going to make it?'

'He's built like a front-row forward. Last I heard there was some improvement in his condition.'

'She told me there's been some deterioration.'

'What did she want from you, Frank?'

He shook his head. 'She said she wanted you and me to work together.'

'What's wrong with that?'

'I don't know what you're doing—not really. I never do.'

'And I don't know that you're doing anything, except that you must be doing something because you're here and giving me the look.'

'The look?'

'The look that says I'm more trouble than I'm worth. Am I, Frank?'

'I can never decide. Sorry, no, I don't mean that.'

'Just like I didn't mean it when I accused you of protecting your pension.'

He burst out into a laugh that was louder and lasted longer than it needed to and the tension between us dropped away.

'So we're quits on insults. My pension's safe because I'm working with a task force that's targeting the GCU, past and present, and it's a delicate operation, as you can imagine. Now what the fuck are you doing and what have you got to drink?'

Over a bottle of cheap red wine we exchanged information. I told him about Hawes and showed him the note. I gave him the names Greenhall had given me and what little I knew about them. He scribbled them down and didn't comment. He said the task force had been set up almost a year ago because whispers had reached the higher-ups that GCU was dirty in the past and not too clean in the present.

'Was Hawes an inside man for your people?' I asked.

Frank shook his head. 'No, we have a couple but they're proceeding at snail's pace and we're not entirely sure they haven't been got at. Can you quote me that stuff you heard on the voice recording?'

'Not exactly. The name Chas was mentioned. Whoever Chas was talking to had killed someone and was looking to kill someone else—to eliminate someone who was . . . ratshit, that's it. And would talk.'

'Is that all?'

'It was just a snippet. There were two disks. God knows how much stuff was on them.'

'Think hard, Cliff. No other names?'

'No.'

'You sure? Nothing more?'

'Let me think . . . meetings—there was talk of a meeting. The other voice said Chas used to love meetings. Then they laughed.'

Frank leaned back in his chair and took a slug of the rough red. 'It's something to go on. I'll put it to our analysts.'

'Analysts?'

'They tease out meanings from whatever information we give them.'

'I could use one.'

'You wouldn't understand a word they say. The stuff Hawes got on to is crucial but if we put a guard on him in the hospital word could get back and people could run for cover.'

'How could they hide?'

'By applying pressure. That's how a cover is kept in place—promotions, demotions, pensions past and present, postings good and bad. There's lots of ways.'

I poured the last of the wine. 'You haven't mentioned politicians.'

'I mention politicians as seldom as I can.'

We were back on comfortable terms although I was aware Frank had avoided some areas. Such as the role of Timothy Greenhall in the whole business. He knew I'd want to protect my client as far as possible and I knew his overriding concern was for the health of the police service. Those objectives could mean some mutually understood lifting of the carpet and sweeping. So far so good, but I knew the really hard question for me was coming up and I had a corresponding one for him.

'What have you done about finding this Constable Carter?' Frank asked.

'Have you ever heard of a lawyer named Soames-Wetherell?'

'Yes.'

'What do you think of him?'

'What does it matter what I think of him? Don't tell me you've been talking to him about all this stuff.'

'No.'

'Well?'

'I'd still like to know your opinion of him.'

'He's erratic but not the worst of them. A good advocate

when he's got material to work with and he's in the mood, but I can't see how he'd help you find someone.'

'Not him, his nephew, name of Paul.'

Ever the copper, Frank said, 'Paul who?'

'Soames or Wetherell, take your pick.'

'Jesus, Cliff, what is he? One of your dodgy PIA mates?'

'No, he's a bikie, aspiring to be the leader of the Bravados.'

18

'A bikie?'

'No ordinary bikie, Frank. This guy's got a degree and military service behind him.'

'A lot of them are ex-army, it's part of the trouble.'

'There are signs that someone from the old GCU might have offed Dusty Miller. Paul's keen to know the truth. I spent some time with the bikies recently, not voluntarily.'

'Funny you didn't mention your bikie connection earlier.' He studied me, looking for cuts and bruises. 'How come they didn't work you over?'

'A couple of them wanted to but I discouraged them. They weren't ex-military, just slow and dumb. Paul sort of eased my way out.'

'Paul? You're buddies?'

'No, I'm using him and he's using me.'

I explained about getting the Bravados to watch for Cathy Carter and to report to me when she was located.

Frank listened with a sceptical look on his face. I smiled at him and he knew what was coming next. He reached for his empty glass.

'Should I open another bottle, Frank?'

'Better not.'

'Okay, your turn to come clean. What can you tell me about Charlie, Tony, Luke and Rooster?'

He sighed. 'I knew Charlie Henderson. He was a desk man, an organiser, not a front-line copper. He wasn't long in the GCU, too old. He retired before the shake-up. Cantello went out under a cloud, excessive force accusations, I think. I suppose he got his super but it wouldn't have been that much. He was a late intake and low level the whole time he was in.'

Frank glanced at his scribbled list. 'I've never heard of Soames.'

'Which suggests what?'

He shrugged. 'Deep undercover, most likely.'

'I'm told he disappeared.'

'They do. That's what they're good at, among other things.'

'Rooster?'

'I think you know something about him from the tone of your voice.'

'A bit. Guesswork. How bad was he?'

Frank swayed from side to side, almost rocking in the chair, which wouldn't have stood up to it. 'Do you know how hard this is to do, Cliff?'

'Of course I do. Ninety-nine point something of police these days are honest public servants. Most of them aren't too bright because they don't have to be. They do shitty jobs and see dreadful things and it's a wonder more of them don't go off the rails. They mostly don't eat their guns like the Americans, but they suffer.'

He nodded. 'Quite a lot get out as soon as they can and they have bad habits and bad attitudes towards society in general.'

'I know, I've met a few of them. Then there are the bad apples, the very bad apples. Is that what Fowler was?'

Frank nodded. 'Grantley Fowler was one of the worst. Behind the matey nickname that made him sound like a man of the people, he hid a very complex personality. He was a chameleon—brutally tough in one context and incredibly sophisticated and smooth in another. He probably stole a couple of million and was responsible for quite a few murders. He was supposed to have bashed someone to death with a torch he'd had specially weighted.'

That fitted with what Cathy had said about the attack on Hawes.

'I'd never heard of him until I checked the web. He didn't seem like such a big fish.'

My kitchen chairs aren't that comfortable but that wasn't why Frank got up and started to pace. It was embarrassment and anger.

'This gets right down to it. Fowler got a deal. He went up for perjury and other pretty low-level charges. He did very soft time under protection.'

'Why?'

'Three reasons. His actual crimes were so bad that if they'd been revealed the papers like the old *National Times* would have had a field day with the police and we were already on the nose just then. There was no law allowing the confiscation of assets acquired through crime then either and Fowler had property, bank accounts and investments all safeguarded by lawyers.'

Frank stopped pacing.

'What's reason three?' I said.

'He had things on senior people in the force and on politicians.'

I still had half a glass of wine left. I swilled it down and shook my head. 'Very interesting, Frank, and it looks as though Greenhall ran into him at some point and benefited somehow, at least in the short term. But if Fowler got away almost scot-free with millions, he's too big to be involved in the present stuff. It's nasty and generates money, but not on the scale you're talking about.'

'That was then, this is now. Our information is that Fowler lost out big time in the GFC and in addition he got badly burned somehow, possibly by a woman. Our analyst says that's a guess based on a large amount of data on corporate collapses. Don't ask me to explain it, because I can't. I told you what they're like. The point is, our work to date suggests that a cash-strapped Fowler, old though he is, could be back in the game. That's why it's so important to get hold of this Hawes material.'

'It could've been Fowler talking to Henderson?'

'Our voice experts would know. We have Fowler on tape from back in the day.'

'Voices change over time.'

'They have ways of compensating for that.'

'Jesus, Frank, all this high-powered technology and it comes down to stuff that came my way because I did some basic spadework for a client.'

'There's other things going on. This is just a strand.'

'That's no comfort.'

'Since when did you expect comfort?'

He was right. I was seldom in what they call the comfort zone, and when I was it was probably because I didn't really know what was happening or wasn't doing the job right.

'So what d'you want to do, Frank? I wouldn't advise staking out the hospital with police. Cathy Carter's pretty smart and well trained. She'd spot them in no time.'

'And she won't spot bikies?'

'I'm pretty sure Paul won't have them in their colours or riding Harleys.'

'You seem to put a lot of faith in this guy.'

'I do. You should meet him.'

'Maybe I will and I hope it's not in court or somewhere worse.'

'What was Fowler's reputation with women?'

'Why?'

'Just a thought.'

I knew Frank wasn't going to tell me about the other irons the task force had in the fire. I knew why he couldn't. And he knew I wouldn't give him every scrap of information or every half-idea I had. It was the kind of mutual understanding we'd reached before and so far it hadn't turned out too badly.

'Fowler was a good-looking bloke, about as tall as you and with much the same build. Dark like you, but without the rough edges.'

'Thanks a lot.'

'He was a womaniser—twice married and with a string of other relationships during, between and after his marriages.'

What women? I wondered. There were certainly enough of them in this case. Kate Greenhall had said her mother was hot for uniforms; Alicia Troy had worked at the Police and Justice Museum. I needed more arrows and dots in my diagrams.

I said, 'I take it no one knows his whereabouts now.'

'Right. If you find out . . .'

'I know, approach with caution.'

He shook his head. 'Look, with all that's happening the pressure's going to reach him. He'll kill you as soon as look at you if it suits him. Be smart for once, Cliff. Stay in touch, close in touch. I have to go.'

Frank left and I located Alicia Troy's number and sent her a text asking to see her as soon as convenient. An answer came back almost straight away that she already had a bottle of the Houghton's waiting for me and she'd see me at 6 pm.

'I know. I never thought you did.'

She released my hand and sipped her wine. 'Of course you did. You suspected every one of the five million people in the fucking city.'

I laughed and had a drink of the wine without having any idea of how it tasted. 'Except you.'

'Including me and your grandmother.' She stood and smoothed her dress. 'You've got an unattached look. How long have you been sleeping alone?'

I stood and moved towards her. 'Too long,' I said.

'Same here. Much too long. It's a well-known fact that losing a partner leaves you randy.'

19

Our love-making was moderately successful, which satisfied us. We were both too experienced to have unreasonably high expectations. The sheets and blankets on her bed were not violently disturbed. She grabbed a couple of tissues and eased the condom from me.

'That was nice,' she said.

'Very nice.'

'Mmm.'

I kissed her, trying not to do damage to her pale, fine-pored skin with my bristles. 'Alicia. It suits you.'

She propped herself up on an elbow. Her breasts were large but firm, blue-veined with dark, spreading nipples. 'Meaning?'

'It's unusual.'

'I'm unusual, all right. I've broken a lot of rules.'

'That's what I mean. You seem to say what you want and do what you want.'

'That's unusual?'

'I reckon. A lot of people, sometimes I think most, are running scared. They're scared to be who they really are, or to do what they really want to do. They're pretending to themselves and everyone else.'

'That's too harsh,' she said. 'I think you're working from an unrepresentative sample, but it's interesting and I'll think about it.'

I reached for her but she wriggled away.

'Don't push your luck,' she said. 'Let's get back to our wine and you can get around to telling me why you're here, apart from wanting to fuck me.'

She poured a bit of wine into her glass and tasted it. 'Warm and stale,' she said. 'I'll cook with it.'

She opened another bottle and got fresh glasses.

'I can't decide whether you were right or not,' I said.

'About what?'

'About wanting to fuck you, but I'm glad you were willing and that we did.'

'I was more than willing. Now, about the other thing.'

'You suggested that Patrick might not have been Timothy Greenhall's son. You implied his wife was unfaithful.'

'That's right. I told you I got that from Patrick. It was just one of the many things that screwed him up. I didn't believe it, though. Why does it matter?'

I told her something of what had happened since our first meeting—the violence, and the questions that needed answering. About why, probably, Patrick had been murdered and what I was trying to do about it and how I had some allies.

She listened in silence, sipping her wine. When I paused she spoke quietly. 'I believed it was suicide.'

'I know you did. Some people are very good at making it look that way. But it was murder and now Timothy Greenhall wants the murderer punished.'

'Does he really have doubts about his paternity?'

'I don't know. The subject didn't come up, but it's important now we might have a connection between Fowler and Patrick's mother. That's why I wanted you to tell me everything you know about her.'

'I don't see why.'

'The suspect's whereabouts are unknown. Shit, I'm sounding like a policeman.'

'Just ask the question.'

'Did Patrick ever say anything about his mother and her . . . interest in uniforms?'

We were sitting on the couch nursing our glasses. She had her long legs tucked up the way women do and was turned sideways. I reached out and stroked her dark hair, in which a touch of grey was just starting to appear. It increased her appeal to me. She took a let-me-think drink.

'I didn't realise there was so much psychology in your line of work, Cliff.'

'From time to time.'

'Uniforms . . . police . . . there's something . . . Yes, I've got it. One of the therapists Patrick went to hypnotised him to recover memories. He said the therapist told him that he had recounted a childhood memory of seeing his mother naked with a man who had a blue uniform jacket thrown over a chair.'

'Did that traumatise him?'

'It would, wouldn't it? But there was a lot going on. He knew his mother and father were at odds with each other and it was just a bit of confirmation. Something else intrigued him though.'

'What was that?'

'He said the therapist told him that under hypnosis he also remembered hearing his mother groaning and saying something about a cock crowing.'

'What did Patrick make of that?'

'Obviously, that it had something to do with his sexual insecurity. But that was central to everything he thought and felt so he didn't attach particular importance to it. I tried to find out if there was anything in Freud about sex and roosters but there wasn't. Why, do you make anything of it?'

I did, but I didn't tell her so. She whipped up curried mince with rice and peppers plus sweet mango chutney and poppadums. I stayed the night and we made love again in the early morning. Then it was coffee and the awkwardness.

I told Alicia I never knew from one day to the next where I'd be or what I'd be doing. Other women I'd told this to took it as a brush-off and reacted badly. She didn't. She said she had to go to Queensland to negotiate with a family about some old goldfields equipment in their possession and that she had a conference in Canada to attend in about six weeks. I said I'd contact her when I had a clear patch and she said she'd try to fit me in.

'That's a joke,' she said.

I kissed her, being even more careful with the stubble.

'If you find out who killed Patrick, I'd like to know. Otherwise, just be careful around the Glocks.'

I went straight to the office, still unshaven and not showered, reluctant to lose the smell and the feel of her. Timothy Greenhall's deceits were peeling off like onion layers. It didn't take much to imagine an enthusiastic Mrs G emoting about a cock, aka a rooster, crowing in the clinches. Did Greenhall know who'd been her lover? Did he really suspect he wasn't Patrick's father? Did he care?

The connection threw up a couple of other questions. Had Mrs G's association with Fowler continued? If so, for how long? And would she know where he was now? How disturbed was she? Could she be questioned? Only one way to find out. I rang Kate Greenhall in Mount Victoria.

'This is Kate.'

'Cliff Hardy.'

'Ah, yes. Just a minute while I kill a few bugs.'

I'd seen a television report of Dusty Miller's funeral and it gave me an opening remark.

'Did you do the flowers for Dusty?'

'Some of them.'

'Get paid?'

'On the knocker. I'm busy, Mr Hardy. What's on your mind?'

'I'm trying to get to speak with your mother.'

'Why?'

'Pursuing my enquiries into Patrick's death. Your view that he was murdered is firming up.'

'That's interesting. How could Jilly help?'

'Jilly?'

'She wasn't the kind of woman you'd call Mum. She'd hit you if you did, or she'd try to.'

'She might've known some people of interest, as the police say.'

'I'm sure she did. Any people in particular?'

I had to tread delicately. 'Policemen, possibly.'

She laughed. 'Very likely, although I think she preferred army. I can't see why you couldn't ask her. Pose as a publisher and say you want to publish her memoirs.'

'How do I get in to see her? The clinic isn't letting her have visitors. Can you give me an authority or do I . . .?'

'You don't need any authority, Mr Hardy. She's checked herself out of rehab and my father's washed his hands of her. She gave me a call this morning. She's staying at the Four

Winds in Darling Harbour, her favourite home away from home. Handy for you, I think, from your card. Just roll up and buy her a drink, or several drinks. I have to go.'

Families, I thought.

No time like the present. I was looking pretty rough but rock stars stay at the Four Winds and I reckoned no one would think I was out of place, except that I was sober. I locked the office and went down to the street with my mind rehearsing questions for Mrs Greenhall.

A big Bravado was sitting astride his Kawasaki next to my car. I had a vague recollection of him as part of the audience when I took down Brucie's brother.

'Paul says you've got to follow me.'

'Where to? I've got business.'

He shrugged.

'Why?'

'He says he's located the woman.'

No time like the present, but first things first. I nodded and got behind the wheel. He rode off, sedately for a bikie, and I guessed Paul had instructed him to be civilised. It looked as if Paul was getting a handle on things, as he'd planned. He could have phoned me with the address but I assumed he wanted to demonstrate his authority to me and his comrades.

I could sense the bikie's impatience as he waited for lights and refrained from burning off slow drivers. We picked up

Parramatta Road in Annandale and threaded our way through Summer Hill to Ashfield. I hadn't been there often and was surprised at the length of the shopping centre and the ethnic diversity. It was an area where big, stately houses still stood but their front fences held multiple letterboxes. Otherwise it was dominated by blocks of flats, mostly red brick. The bikie pulled up in front of one of these and killed his engine. He took off his helmet, turned to me and pointed.

Paul was standing fifty yards away on the other side of the street. He was in the full Bravados regalia and there was a nest of motorbikes drawn up neatly beside him but no riders in sight. He beckoned to me but I wasn't having that. I leaned back against the car and looked up and down the street. A few struggling trees, a lot of parked cars, a slow trickle of traffic. Paul shrugged and approached.

'She came this morning,' he said. 'Looked very distressed.' He pointed to a block of flats opposite and a little way down the street. 'She's in there, second-floor front, number four. The woman with her checked the letterbox before they went in.'

I nodded at the bikes. 'Where're your brothers?'

'Posted. There's a back and side exit.'

'You've done a good job.'

'Wasn't that hard. I'll leave you to it. Contact me with whatever you find out.'

He walked away and he and my escort started their bikes simultaneously. The roar brought two other Bravados from their positions and the four of them took off. I waited until the noise had died away and the exhaust smoke had cleared and approached the entrance to the flats. I pushed the button for number four.

'Who is it?'

'My name's Hardy. Cathy knows me. It's important that I speak to her.'

There was a pause and then the release on the door sounded. I went in and up the stairs. The door to flat four was open and a woman was standing there. She was older than Cathy but bore some resemblance, a sister or a cousin perhaps.

'She wants to know how you found her.'

'I had someone watching. I know she's distressed and I think I know why. I want to help if I can.'

She stepped aside to let me in. 'I doubt if you can, but she's willing to see you, briefly.'

She led me through to a bedroom that was in half-darkness. Cathy was sitting on the bed propped up by pillows. Even in the poor light I could see that her face was puffy and her eyes were blinking away a new bout of tears brought on by my arrival. I sat on the bed and waited.

She sniffed and wiped her eyes with the back of her hand. 'He had a series of major brain aneurisms overnight,' she said. 'He was still alive, but they said there was virtually no brain function at all. Colin was an orphan,' she said. 'He didn't have any family. There was no one else to do it.'

I nodded.

'I gave them the authority to turn off the life support at 4 am. He wasn't ever going to be . . .'

'I'm sorry,' I said. 'He was a good man.'

'He was a bloody fool.'

'We have to stop them.'

She gave a strangled laugh. 'That's why you're here, isn't it? You want the disks.'

'I'm here because I was worried about you. But yes, I want the disks. We have to stop them.'

'They're gone.'

'What?'

'I destroyed them. I snapped them in half and then again. Look, I cut myself.'

She showed me her bandaged right hand.

She was sobbing now, her shoulders jerking. 'I don't care about those bastards. I don't care about you. I don't care about anything.'

20

Janice, Cathy's cousin, said she'd look after her and that she'd recover.

'We're not a suicidal lot, we Carters,' she said.

I said that was good to know and left my card, telling her to contact me if there was anything I could help Cathy with.

Back in the car I rang Frank Parker to tell him that Colin Hawes was dead and that his information was no longer available. He swore and repeated his advice to be careful.

My next call was to Paul but I got an answer service telling me that the subscriber wasn't available and that I could leave a brief message that would be transmitted as a text. I didn't bother. I couldn't anticipate his reaction and felt I had to speak to him, preferably person to person, to prevent a misunderstanding and to deal with his anger. How our association was going to play out from this point I had no idea.

I decided to go home and clean up before tackling Mrs Greenhall at the Four Winds. I needed some time to recover from the loss of Hawes, whom I'd liked, and my disappointment at the destruction of the disks. I also had to frame questions and possibly lies. And I had medication to take. The traffic had thickened and with part of the route unfamiliar because I'd simply been following the bikie, I had to concentrate on my driving and put everything else on hold.

Approaching home I kept an eye out for bikies or police but saw none. I felt sad about Hawes as I unlocked my door, as if the spirit of his unexpected presence there had lingered. Going inside I reflected that both Hawes and Cathy had been here and that I hadn't done any good for either of them. With Hawes dead, assuming the people I was after had also killed Dusty Miller and Patrick Greenhall, that was three strikes against them and plenty of motivation for me.

The Four Winds had started out as a rival to the Novotel but had gone down a few notches. It still had the tinted glass, steel and marble and the plants in pots but the steel had a dull look and some of the plants had wilted. But the staff were clinging to their pretensions and I was glad I'd worn one of my two suits. The absence of a tie marked me as a free spirit. The male receptionist was in a smart, military-style uniform, perhaps part of the appeal of the place for Mrs Greenhall.

'I believe you have a Mrs Timothy Greenhall staying here.'

He didn't have to check. 'Yes, sir.'

'Would you know whether she's in?'

His expression was a Costello-style smirk. He inclined his head to the left. 'I believe Mrs Greenhall is in the bar.'

He'd dropped the 'sir', which I knew meant something.

There were two people at the bar and a few at tables but the lone woman had to be her. She was sitting at a table in the dimmest light in the place. She had pewter-coloured hair nicely styled and in that light could have passed for forty although she had to be ten years older. Careful makeup, discreet jewellery, a low-necked silk dress showing cleavage between pushed-up breasts. The long cigarette she drew on glowed electronically and the vapour she blew out was odourless. A bottle of champagne stood in an ice bucket. Her glass was half full, the other glass on the table was empty.

'Darling,' she said. 'You're a little late. Jilly was getting a teensy bit worried. Sit down and have a sip while we get acquainted.'

It wasn't a hard situation to grasp, given what I'd been told about her. I sat and topped up her glass and poured some for myself.

She leaned forward, squinted and then seemed to realise that, while leaning forward gave a better view of her cleavage, squinting produced lines and wrinkles she didn't need. 'Jeremy, isn't it? My, you're big. A little older than I expected but, hey, I mentioned maturity, didn't I? And experience counts. Youth is wasted on the young. Am I right?'

'Absolutely . . . Jilly. Happy days and nights.'

'Let's not get ahead of ourselves, sweetie. Although . . .' I felt her leg brush against mine under the table, 'I must say I'm feeling quite excited already. There's chemistry here; I can feel it, can't you?'

'I believe you're right.'

The electronic cigarette sat neglected in the ashtray as she smoothed her dress with both hands.

'You remind me of . . . Drink up and we'll go to my room and play with our chemical . . . chemistry sets.'

She was quite drunk and the laugh that was meant to tinkle was brittle and a little wheezy. She dropped the electronic cigarette and the pack into her patent leather bag.

'I hate those bloody things but what can a girl do? D'you smoke, darling? Of course you do. You all do. We can puff away on my balcony.'

She knocked back the champagne in two gulps and I did the same. She stood and, like any experienced drunk, made steadying herself with a hand on the table seem like a natural gesture. She was quite small but her extravagantly high heels brought her up to about average height. Her dress had a layered, slightly flared knee-length skirt. Her legs were good. She shepherded me out of the bar and across the lobby, talking animatedly about nothing at all and just occasionally leaning against me for orientation and support.

We reached the lifts and she stood, humming softly and adjusting the shoulder strap of her bag. The adjustment caused the neckline of her dress to dip a little further, revealing black lace. We stepped into the lift; she glanced at herself in the mirror and looked away quickly. Under the harsh light she aged but the foundations of what had once been real beauty were still there. She glanced up at my well-worn features and seemed to feel reassured as she squeezed my arm. Just for a second I wondered how the real Jeremy would cope down in the bar. I didn't feel good about what was happening, but then, I hadn't been able to come up with a promising way of approaching her, and luck's a fortune, as they say.

We reached her floor and got out with her leaning heavily against me now. She dipped into her bag and came up with the card. She handed it to me.

'Be a gentleman, darling. I love a gentleman.'

I got the door open and stood aside to let her in. She went by me in a waft of perfume and wine breath and made straight for the balcony. She bumped into a chair but stayed upright and got the glass door open. She had a cigarette in her mouth and the lighter clicking before I was halfway into the suite. It had all the high-dollar fittings—the carpet, the mirrors, the leather—but, like the hotel itself, it showed signs of wear and tear. Magazines in the rack looked a bit tattered and one of the curtains sagged where its ring had given way.

'Scotch, darling,' she said. 'Let's have some lovely scotch from the lovely little bottles. Doubles. While I find you your . . .'

She started to fish in her bag and swore as she dropped her cigarette. She let it burn out on the tiles and slumped into a chair as if the fresh air and tobacco combination had hit her like an anaesthetic. I went to the mini-bar, took out four miniature bottles of Dewar's, cracked some ice cubes into a glass and put the lot on a tray with two glasses.

When I got to the balcony she had another cigarette going in a shaky hand and there was a scattering of banknotes on the table. Her dress had hoicked up above her knees, either by accident or design, but her eyes were half closed and I guessed the bottle of champagne in the bar hadn't been her first while waiting for Jeremy.

'You're a darling, darling,' she said as I put the tray down and sat opposite her.

I put ice in the two glasses and poured the scotch.

She giggled. 'So deft. So masterful.'

I had a problem. If she drank the scotch she'd almost certainly pass out, but if I told her who I was and tried to question her there was no telling what her reaction would be. I watched apprehensively as she took a solid sip.

I shuffled the money into a neat pile. 'You said I reminded you of someone, Jilly. Who was that?'

I couldn't help thinking of the Stones' song 'Far Away Eyes'. Under the influence of alcohol and God knows what medications, she wasn't really here. She was somewhere in her swirling, happy, hopeful, sad past.

'Rooster,' she said. 'You look like my Rooster . . .'

She shocked me then by doing an imitation of a clucking hen.

'I loved Rooster,' she said. 'I gave him everything he asked for.'

'Yes?'

'Yes, yes, yes to everything he wanted. Every way to do it he wanted, every way . . .'

'I'm sorry.'

'You're sorry, everybody's sorry. He'll be sorry. I know where he is, the bastard.'

I tried to keep my voice light and non-threatening, dis-interested. 'Where is he, Jilly? Where's Rooster?'

She was deep into her disturbed memories now and scarcely aware of me at all as she took a shaky drag on a fresh cigarette and a slug of her drink. 'Rooster's a stud and he's got a stud farm 'cos he's a stud and a son of a gun.'

'Oh, yes. Where?'

'Camden. Ever been to Camden, Jerry, sweetie?'

'I have.'

She giggled and tossed back the rest of her drink. 'Jilly hasn't been there, Jerry. Nobody's been there, but Jilly knows . . .'

Her head fell forward and she slumped in the chair. The cigarette fell from her fingers into her lap. I snatched it up but not before it had left a scorch mark on her dress. She tried to lift her head but couldn't. 'Sorry,' she mumbled. 'Sorry, Jerry.'

A breeze sprang up just as she started to snore. It didn't move a hair of her lacquered head but it disturbed the notes on the table so that they fluttered down onto the tiles. I waited until her breathing became regular and lifted her from the chair. She was feather-light, thin everywhere, and her small, elegant shoes fell off and looked sad down there with the burned-out cigarette and the money.

I carried her to the bedroom and laid her on the bed. I filled a glass with water and put it on the table beside her and drew the curtain to dim the room. Then I left.

21

Not my finest hour, but you play the hand you're dealt and I now had a sort of fix on Fowler. How many stud farms were there in the Camden area? Could be a few, but I had acquaintances, from the times I used to try landing daily doubles, who'd probably know all about them. It was one of those moments you work for in any investigation—when pieces of information intersect and you get a point to focus on.

The questions were: who would I share this with—Frank, Paul, Greenhall? And how useful would it be knowing where Fowler was without evidence of his role in the deaths of Patrick Greenhall, Dusty Miller and Colin Hawes? I'd read a fair bit of military history in my time, particularly about the medieval Hundred Years War. In those days, unlike now, the kings or the leaders of the country turned up on the battlefield to direct operations. They took a chance and some were killed, like Richard III, but they were surrounded by supporting knights ready to escort them to safety if things went wrong. Mostly, when kings were captured or killed, they were betrayed by a supporter changing sides at the crucial moment.

As I drove back to the office my mind kept flicking to my recollection of Hawes's phone tap. Assuming 'Chas' was Charlie Henderson, the one named by Greenhall, there was no way to tell who he was talking to without the disk and someone able to identify the voice. Was it Fowler? Possibly. In any case it was someone who had killed and planned to kill again, but there was no time frame. No way to tell when Hawes had made the recording. The unknown voice had said 'Chas' had loved meetings and Frank had said that Henderson had been a desk man. He'd sounded nervous, a possible weak link. But how to find him? It was a common enough name and nothing had come up on the web about him. Frank was the obvious person to ask but I didn't want to put any more pressure on him at this stage.

What did retired senior police officers do? If they didn't go north for the sun and the Fourex they sailed or joined flash golf clubs. I needed a hacker and I knew a good one but he'd cost a lot of money. I still had a fair bit of the cash I'd drawn to bribe Miller but it was shrinking and I'd need more. I phoned Greenhall and told him I needed five thousand dollars.

'You're still buying me time to get this new thing off the ground and I'm grateful. What do you need the money for?'

'To track Charlie Henderson.'

'Did he kill my son?'

'I don't think so.'

'I agree with you. Not the type.'

'But I think he knows who did.'

'It's on its way to your account.'

Nils Olquist was a Finn who'd worked for Nokia and Apple and had pursued an Australian girl to Sydney where he'd married her and decided to stay. He'd worked as an IT consultant for the police, ICAC and various media organisations. I'd found his fourteen-year-old daughter after she'd done a flit with her boyfriend. She'd regretted it and the boyfriend had become violent and possessive. I'd persuaded him to let the girl go and shown him the error of his ways without too much trouble for me and minimal damage to him. Nils had been pleased and we'd stayed in touch, having a drink now and then and sharing an interest in boxing.

I rang him and agreed to meet him at what he called his bunker in Erskineville. Nils had made money and invested well and he'd bought a disused warehouse and turned it into a spacious high-tech living and working area. It had state-of-the-art security, which took a few minutes to penetrate. Then I was met by Nils at the top of the stairs that led to his workspace.

No weedy IT geek, Nils stood about 190 centimetres and would've weighed a hundred kilos. Ethnically, he was a mixture of Swedish and Finnish and claimed a family connection to Ingemar Johansson, briefly the heavyweight boxing champion of the world.

For all his height and bulk, Nils was a gentle, almost childish soul who delighted in hacking for fun. When we met over a beer he'd often open with his latest prank penetration and interference with an IT system he disapproved of—a right-to-life mob or an anti-asylum seeker group. He was a committed left-winger.

We shook hands and I followed him into a world I had no understanding of: at least six computers were arrayed beside a similar number of screens and charging decks for multiple mobile phones. Lights blinked and machines hummed and Nils, seeing my confusion, mimed an orchestral conduction.

'It all makes sense, Cliff,' he said.

'To you. I'm glad.'

'It freaks you, I can tell. To my office for a talk and a drink, yes?'

Bloody aquavit, I thought. *Have to watch myself.*

The office was partitioned off, small and comfortable. Nothing serious happened here. Nils opened the bar fridge and poured two small glasses full of clear liquid. The ritual was that the first one went down immediately and it was social after that.

'So, Cliff,' Nils said. 'I owe you.'

He did. I'd done the work for him pro bono before he'd started making money and he was always asking how he could repay me. This was the first time I'd asked to see him at his place of work. His time had come and he knew it.

'We'll get to it,' I said. 'How's Trudie?'

'In school and doing well. Thanks to you.'

'Only partly. I need a favour, Nils—a hacking job.'

'Yes?'

'The police pension plan. Can you get into it?'

He studied what was left in his glass as if it wasn't nearly enough. 'Jesus, Cliff.'

'Not to steal from it. Just to look at one individual and see how he's fixed financially and get an address and phone numbers. Email, too, if you can.'

Nils relaxed. 'Well, I suppose . . .'

'Five grand, Nils. Cash, fun money.'

I knew that Nils was meticulous about his finances; working for a diverse range of employers and earning a lot of money he had to keep a careful watch on his tax obligations. He ran his hands through his thick white-blond hair and then stared at them as if imagining them clicking the keys.

'How urgent?' he said.

'Very.'

'Give me the name.'

I reached for my notebook and he shook his head.

'Nothing on paper.'

'Charles Henderson. Resigned as something like super-intendent . . . say, ten years ago.'

'Okay. That's all you want? Finances, an address, phones and email? You don't want me to hack the phones?'

'Don't tempt me. No.'

'I could. Why not?'

'This is heavy stuff, mate. I want you in and out and no trace.'

He nodded. 'I'll send you an encrypted email. Let's call the password Ingemar. Okay?'

I lifted my glass and spoke the only word of Finnish I knew, thanks to Nils. '*Kippis.*'

As I half expected, Paul was waiting for me when I got back to the office. He got out of a VW Golf and I did a double-take. He was wearing a well-cut dark suit over a black skivvy and looked like an executive in a go-ahead commercial organisation of some kind. The bushy hair was tightly bunched and he was clean-shaven with the sideburns trimmed back. He came across the road to me with a smile spreading across his face.

'What's wrong, Hardy? Never seen a suit before?'

'Who's dead?' I said.

He laughed. 'No one. I've been to see Uncle Arthur. I like to show him my serious side. You've been very busy, I'm told. Time we had a talk.'

We went up to the office. It clearly failed to impress him as he settled in the chair, taking care of the crease in his trousers.

He raised two fingers to tick items off. 'A visit to the Four Winds hotel in Darling Harbour and one to Erskineville to an IT expert. Don't tell me you didn't learn anything from all this gadding about.'

'You've got a great network. How are you going at keeping it all together?'

'As Ringo said, it don't come easy, but I'm relying on you to help. Let's cut to the chase. Who killed Dusty?'

'I have to think about this. D'you want some coffee?'

'Not particularly.'

'I do. I've just had two shots of aquavit and need to clear my head.'

'And you drove? That was stupid.'

'It was and I don't want to compound the mistake.'

He unbuttoned his jacket and relaxed in the chair as if he hadn't a worry in the world. 'Take your time.'

I made the coffee, weighing up how much to tell him, how much to trust him, and the hardest part—trying to think ahead to the possible consequences of whatever I said. I needed to know more about his intentions before I revealed anything. I put the plastic cup of coffee on the desk in front of him.

'No milk,' I said.

'No worries.' But he didn't move to take the cup.

I went back behind the desk. 'Suppose I tell you I've got a possible target, but no proof and I don't know where he is—what would you say?'

'I'd say you weren't telling me the whole truth.'

'Suppose I said I was working on a way to get the proof through another person, an accomplice, you might say.'

He reached for the coffee, took a sip, made a face and put the cup back. 'That's terrible coffee. Was that deliberate?'

I shrugged. 'My coffee always turns out bitter. I don't know why.'

He stretched like a cat and seemed to feel happier for doing it, the way a cat does. 'You know, I'm enjoying this,' he said. 'Don't get much of a chance for verbal chess with the brothers.'

'How's Brucie?'

'He's okay, the poor bastard, but like the others, he's not much for hypotheticals. To answer your question, I'd say that if you give me the name of the possible target as a gesture of good faith, I'd be willing to help you work for the proof through the other guy—for a time at least.'

'I'll be frank with you, Paul. I don't want you to kill the man I have in mind. I'd want him tried, convicted and sent away.'

'Agreed.'

'That easy?'

'I told you I have long-range plans. I don't need a murder charge or anything like it.'

'Grantley "Rooster" Fowler,' I said. 'Corrupt cop. A killer who negotiated a deal because he had a lot of dirt on others higher up. Said to have money. He did some soft time and now he's dropped out of sight. But still active . . . possibly.'

'But you know where to look.'

'Maybe, but as I say, I've got no proof. So I want to come at it sideways through this other bloke.'

'Who is?'

'I'll hold on to that until I hear from my IT guy.'

'Not a lot of mutual trust in all this, is there?'

'What did you expect?'

'Just about what I'm getting. But I may have a surprise in store for you.'

'I don't like surprises.'

'No, you prefer to be in control, like me, but you're not in control of this, are you?'

'Not yet.'

He laughed. 'And you won't be, without my help. I can tell you that, Hardy, for certain.'

He stood and buttoned his jacket. 'By the way, you never told me why that woman you had me follow was so upset.'

'Her husband had been murdered.'

He nodded. 'That'd do it. Was this Fowler involved?'

'It had the hallmarks.'

He headed for the door. 'That's the worst coffee I've ever tasted.'

'It's pretty bad in prison.'

'You'd know. I wouldn't, and won't ever.'

'You sure?'

'Pretty sure. We'll be in touch, Hardy. I just might have something for you before you have anything for me.'

He went out, closing the door quietly behind him. His calm confidence verged on the unnerving and I sat in my chair drinking the foul coffee with my mind almost a blank. Paul was one of those people you feel are trying, physically and mentally, to climb over you to get where they want to be. You have to either let them do it or pull them down, and it's hard, either way.

22

Perce Tresize had done just about everything there was to do in the horse-racing business. He'd been a jockey, an owner and breeder, a trainer and a punter.

'My tragedy,' he once told me, 'was that I wasn't quite good enough at any of my racing activities, especially the betting.'

Perce's father had been an SP bookie who'd told him that betting on horses was a mug's game. Like many sons, Perce had set out to prove his father wrong and failed. Whatever assets he'd accumulated from riding and owning horses he'd lost at betting on them. These days he wrote an ill-paid racing column for a newspaper and occasionally appeared as a comedy character, 'Percy the punter', on a morning television show. He had a good line of patter and was amusing company in small doses.

I usually drank at the Toxteth in Glebe. Perce preferred the pub that used to be called the Ancient Briton but now just goes by the name the AB Hotel, and he could be found there most nights talking racing to anyone inclined to listen. Pint-sized, Perce was a two-pot screamer who could make a middy last an hour and a schooner last all night.

It was Sunday-night quiet at the AB when I arrived and I found Perce nursing a middy of Old and picking at a steak sandwich. He'd told me that the only way for a jockey to keep his weight down was to keep his gob shut and from doing it for so long he'd lost his appetite.

'Hello, Perce,' I said. 'Here, I'll help you out.'

I took two chips from his plate and ate them.

'Cliff Hardy,' he said, 'still got your sense of humour, I see.'

'I retain that, Perce, as you do.'

'I hope so. Still leaving the daily doubles to the mugs?'

'Absolutely. That's how I have five hundred bucks to offer you for some information.'

He groaned. 'Not about a horse.'

'No, about a stud out at Camden.'

Perce sipped beer and ate a small mouthful. 'There's a few of them.'

'I know. I checked on the web. They're all wonderful with their green grass and white fences and the shit of their horses doesn't smell.'

He grinned. 'That's about right.'

'Ownership'd be hard to trace?'

'Right again.'

'Can you think of one set up a while ago, late nineties,

say. Low-profile, doesn't do much, possibly a front for other activities?'

'You're slandering the fair name of the racing industry.'

'Yeah.'

Perce lost all interest in his food and pushed the plate away. He took a gulp of beer. 'Five hundred? Could you see your way to a grand?'

'Might.'

He looked around to be sure no one was in earshot. 'There's a Camden operation I've wondered about. Don't know anything specific, mind, but a while back there was a bit of a doping scandal. Nothing much, and it didn't reach the stewards. It was more talk and rumour among the . . . what's that Italian word?'

'Cognoscenti.'

'That's it. Must use that in my column. But I did hear that a couple of the people talking about it got sat on pretty heavily.'

'Who by?'

'The coppers.'

'I need the name, Perce.'

He rubbed his index finger and thumb together. I'd anticipated him upping the ante and I'd put a thousand of the wad I was carrying in a compartment of my wallet. I fished it out and let Perce see it and no one else. Then I went to the bar and got a glass of red for myself and another middy for Perce.

He accepted the drink. 'Top Gun Bloodstock.'

That clicked with part of Jilly's drunken rambling and I put ten notes, folded tightly, into Perce's hand.

At home I Googled and found the site. It was low-key compared with most of the others. Smaller acreage, more restricted facilities, fewer horses. Most of the stud sites boasted of winners and their winning progeny. Top Gun named a few horses, none of which meant much to me because I hadn't been paying attention to the races for years, apart from an annual bet on the Slipper. Depending on your standards, Top Gun could be described as either modest or struggling. The owner wasn't revealed. The manager was one Tom Hobhouse. Nothing came up in a search for him but I had a feeling I'd heard the name somewhere.

I detected an air of secrecy about the place, or was that just wishful thinking? I liked the smell of police protection and the location safely within the boundaries of Camden. A horse stud located there was a very convenient place to lie low but also keep an eye on things in Sydney and environs. Security staff would be a justifiable adjunct and even firearms to protect the sensitive horses from being spooked by feral animals. I knew I was talking myself into it, but I sensed a breakthrough.

I'd eaten a handful of nuts and drunk the glass of red after I'd paid Perce. We'd chatted. I wasn't hungry. I took my medication with another glass of wine and sat back to think about things. When Nils came in with information on 'Chas' Henderson as I was sure he would, it'd be a matter of applying pressure and choosing my allies. It was a comfortable feeling so I got down on the floor and did a series of push-ups and crunches to banish it.

23

Nothing happened for the next few days. I went to the bank and drew out what I needed for Nils but still hadn't heard from him.

Janice, Cathy Carter's cousin, had invited me to the service for Colin Hawes at Rookwood. I went and stood among the sizeable crowd of mourners—quite a few police, some in uniform, members of Cathy's family, presumably, and a contingent of people from various rowing clubs. No celebrant, which was a relief. A few people spoke, including Cathy, who gave no sign that Hawes's death had been anything other than an accident.

We adjourned to a pub. I tried to work my way towards Cathy but Janice caught my eye and shook her head. A cop I knew vaguely and disliked from some earlier contact approached me.

'Bill McKenzie,' he said.

I nodded. I had a drink in one hand and a sandwich in the other so I didn't have to shake hands.

'Something funny about this?' he said.

'Funny?'

'Wrong word. Odd.'

I sipped my drink. 'Did you know Colin?'

'No.'

'Why're you here, then?'

He turned away slowly. 'Among other things, to wonder why you are,' he said.

Patience has never been my strong suit and I was starting to think of other ways of confirming that I knew where Fowler was, and putting pressure on him, when Paul sprang his surprise.

'I've got someone you have to meet,' he said when he rang.

'Who?'

'When you meet him.'

'Why?'

'Same answer—just ask where and when, Hardy. That's all you need for now.'

This guy was turning out to be a skilled player. It gave me confidence in one way and concern in another. I felt he could probably do what he set out to do, whatever it was. Would he do as he'd said—stay within the bounds of the law? Very hard to say. Would I want him to? Again, hard to say, but I was certainly going to need his help.

'Okay, where and when?'

'Uncle Arthur's office at six this evening.'

'What're we going to do—drink sherry?'

But his nickname should have been 'Last Word'—he was gone.

I was at Soames-Wetherell's office on time. The chambers had emptied apart from a couple of women working in an office amid stacks of paper. Paralegals? Low-status associates? Soames-Wetherell, senior partner, was there in his shirtsleeves; Paul was sitting at the conference table reading a book. He wore a white T-shirt with a V-neck and the jacket of his suit hung on the back of his chair. Another man stood looking out of the window at the city as if he'd never seen it before. He turned around as I came in. Paul slapped the book shut and stood.

'Hardy, this is Luke Soames.'

Soames came towards me. He was tall and thin. He had curling grey hair and a grey beard but wasn't very old—sixty, perhaps, or a well-preserved sixty-five. The skin not covered by the beard was very tanned.

'I see you've heard of me,' he said.

I nodded. I'd resolved to keep as quiet as I could until things became clear.

Arthur Soames-Wetherell said, 'Luke is a second cousin—I think that's the term. He's just back from Thailand.'

I couldn't resist it. 'Once removed,' I said.

Paul shook his head. 'Don't worry, Luke. He makes jokes like that. Thinks he's funny. Sometimes he is.'

The lawyer made an invitational gesture. 'Let's sit down and talk.'

I looked at Paul. 'Where's the sherry?'

Soames wore a lightweight suit cut in the unstructured way Asian tailors can achieve and sensible expatriates prefer, a blue shirt and no tie. He grinned. 'Good idea. How about it, Arthur?'

I took off my jacket and sat, draping the jacket over the chair as Paul had done.

Soames had a sardonic smile he'd obviously worked on. 'No shoulder holster?'

'Ankle strap,' I said.

Soames-Wetherell produced a bottle of Mildara George dry sherry and four glasses. He poured and passed the glasses around. Soames sniffed and drank; I drank without sniffing; Paul ignored the drink.

'Let's cut the bullshit,' Paul said, 'and get down to it.'

'I thought you wanted to be a politician, Paulie—that's what I used to call him when he was a nipper,' Soames said. 'You'd better get used to bullshit. It's there by the ton.'

Paul gave Soames a respectful nod and then turned less respectfully to me. 'I'd been hearing stories about Luke ever since he went missing. When all this business to do with cops and guns came up, a few things clicked. One of my aunts had actually seen Luke in Thailand, or thought she had. I decided to find him and see if he could help us.'

'Lot of people in Thailand,' I said. 'Some of them hiding. How did you find him?'

'Contacts,' Paul said. 'Dusty used to import hash from there and I knew a few names. Who knew other names. It wasn't that hard.'

'Sounds dangerous, though.'

Paul shrugged.

Soames said, 'Paul's right, it wouldn't have been too hard. I've kept my nose clean over there, but people talk and I've probably got careless in recent years.'

Soames-Wetherell sipped his sherry. 'Good passport, Luke?'

'Good enough, apparently.'

'I appreciate that you're taking a risk coming back,' I said. 'I'd like to know how you can help and what you think you'd be helping with.'

'Nailing Rooster Fowler,' Soames said. 'And settling a couple of old scores.'

Paul was one of those people who don't like being left out of the conversation. He tossed off his sherry in one gulp. 'Tell him, Luke.'

Soames folded his arms and looked at the lawyer as if weighing up how much he could allow him to hear. Then he turned his attention to me. 'I heard of you, Hardy, when I was working undercover here back in the last century. The word was that you were a bit wild at times, but capable. When Paul said he had an arrangement with you I was encouraged.'

I didn't need flattery from a corrupt cop. 'I'm waiting to hear about your offer of help. Unless I miss my guess it'll be hedged around with all kinds of conditions.'

'Naturally,' Soames-Wetherell said.

I remembered Harry Tickener's assessment of him and felt it was confirmed. The lawyer was enjoying the by-play of his two relatives and no doubt thinking of ways to keep his distance from whatever might be being talked about and planned, especially if it went wrong.

Soames put both big, sun-damaged hands on the table. 'I have, in a safe place, the torch Fowler used to beat an informer named Roy Carlton to death. It has Carlton's blood and tissue on it, Fowler's fingerprints and also his blood because he split a fingernail in the assault. The DNA of both of them would be as fresh as daisies.'

'Your insurance,' I said.

'Right. Rooster knew I had it and that I was opting out of the mess we'd all got ourselves into. And that if he came after me, which he would certainly otherwise have done, I'd use it against him.'

I was sceptical. 'How many times did he try to get it back from you?'

'A few. Then he ran into his own set of problems and let it drop. He probably hopes I'll die of AIDS.'

None of us felt like taking up that point.

'So why now?' I said.

'I'm in remission from lung cancer. Don't know how long I've got. Could be very soon or a fair way off. I've got arrangements to make for my family in Thailand. I want them to come here. I'd need a clean sheet for that to happen and that means a deal. I help put Fowler away and I get the grateful thanks of the authorities.'

'That's where I can be useful,' Soames-Wetherell said. 'Negotiating.'

'And,' Soames said, 'Paul tells me you have another line of attack. Safety in numbers. I'm guessing you reckon to put the frighteners on one of the old bunch. Am I right?'

'Yes.'

'Who?'

It was boots and all now. Whatever the dangers of cooperation with the likes of Paul and Soames, it was the obvious course to take. Paul was listening attentively.

'Charlie Henderson,' I said.

Soames leaned back in his chair. 'Chas,' he said. 'You couldn't have picked a weaker reed. A real gutless wonder, Chas, but he hopped in for his share when the money was there. What've you got on him?'

I shrugged. 'Virtually nothing. A snatch of recorded phone conversation unhappily no longer physically available. I don't even know where he is, but I've got a guy working on it.'

'Some IT bloke,' Paul said. 'Hacking into his finances is my guess.'

'Everybody's got something to hide, as the boy said. My guy's looking for Henderson's address and phone numbers and also checking his financial situation.'

Soames-Wetherell was alarmed. 'Hacking bank records. That's dangerous. They've got all sorts of traces . . .'

'Not a bank,' I said. 'And best you don't know.'

'I agree.' The lawyer drained his glass and gestured with the bottle. I was the only one who accepted a top-up.

Soames was looking at it from every angle. 'Paul tells me you're hoping to do something for Tommy Greenfall. Is that right?'

'You know him?'

'Pistol shot with him. He was bloody good. Then he was . . . useful in certain ways.'

'I suspect Fowler or someone close to him had the man's son killed to keep the father in line. Greenhall Junior had seen some evidence of his father's connection to your lot and had been indiscreet about it.'

Soames nodded. 'That'd be Rooster's style.'

Paul clearly thought this was straying from the point and he brought us back. 'I get the feeling you know where Fowler is, Hardy,' he muttered. 'You haven't said so but it would've come up if you didn't know.'

On the ball again, I thought. 'I've got a pretty good idea.'

Soames said, 'And, before I popped up, supposing you found Chas and had some useful dope on him, how do *you* plan to induce him to finger Fowler?'

'Hold on,' I said. 'I don't want to appear paranoid but has this place been checked for recording devices?'

Paul gave one of his rare laughs. 'I've been here for a while, right, Uncle Arthur? And I've done a state-of-the-art check. If anyone had any kind of line open it'd be defeated by the whistling from my little box of tricks.'

'All right,' I said, looking at Soames. 'Well, now that I know what you have tucked away, that'd certainly be useful. But I wasn't planning on anything so subtle. I just thought I'd get Paul and the Bravados to scare the living shit out of him.'

part three

24

I explained that I couldn't hurry the information on Henderson. 'I told my guy to be careful and that takes time.'

The lawyer nodded approvingly; the other two were less happy. I decided to turn the screws a little and asked Paul how his authority in the Bravados stood.

He gave me a sour look. 'Okay for now, but I need a result.'

I turned to Soames. 'How're you feeling, Luke? I see you've still got your hair.'

He reached for the sherry bottle. 'They told me you were a smartarse bastard and they were right.' He poured a glass, took a sip and smiled. His face was transformed and I could see the chameleon-like quality in him that must've helped in his undercover days. 'But then again, that's exactly what this situation might need.'

'Where's Fowler?' Paul snapped.

I shook my head. 'All in good time.'

The meeting broke up with each of us establishing contact numbers. I didn't ask where Soames was staying. I was sure he'd be keeping his distance from everyone else and monitoring events rather than taking an active part. When his hour came I was prepared to believe he'd give it all he had and, if it never came, as he'd done before, he'd be gone without a trace.

I'd caught a bus into the city and was heading for the stop when my mobile rang. I didn't recognise the number.

'Hardy.'

'Cliff, this is Alicia.'

I stopped in my tracks. 'Alicia.'

'You sound surprised.'

'No, pleased.'

'Where are you? I tried your home and office numbers first. You're out and about.'

'Macquarie Street.'

'That's good. I was working late and just finished. Could we meet up?'

After the all-male, mistrustful, conspiratorial meeting with its likely highly unpleasant consequences, the thought of seeing her was like a cooling breeze. She proposed a restaurant at Circular Quay. That sounded full of promise and I agreed to meet her there in thirty minutes. I changed direction and strolled down towards the water.

Lower Macquarie Street, opposite the Botanical Gardens, was quiet and dark—mostly office buildings with very little traffic and only one hotel or café per block. I noticed two young men cross from the park side and walk towards me.

'Got a spare smoke, mister?'

Young and no actor this one, tone all wrong, and his mate moved to get around me. I kicked the one who'd spoken hard in the shin. I was wearing solid shoes and a kick just there is crippling. He lurched away swearing and gripped a parking-meter post for support. His mate attempted a clumsy rabbit punch but I ducked it, bullocked him up against a sandstone wall and hit him with two sharp jabs to his left ear. That hurts and doesn't damage the fist of the one doing the hitting. He sat down hard and swore just as his mate had done. Muggers with no talent.

'Do something else,' I said. 'Because you're not too bloody good at this.'

Alicia was wearing her business pants suit, a white shirt and a wide smile as we arrived simultaneously outside the restaurant. We wrapped our arms around each other and kissed hard.

She released me and stepped back. 'Hey, you're supposed to be Mr Keep Your Distance.'

I reached for her. 'Who says?'

'You did.'

'I'm very glad to see you, Alicia.'

She took my arm and we went in. The place was busy but we were shepherded to a table where we could just see the water if we craned our necks.

'Good day?' she said.

'Promising.'

'That can be better than good. What was that I smelled on your breath?'

'Sherry. I was in a conference with a lawyer. Sorry.'

'I didn't mind. It took me back. It was all the go at department parties in my final year at Sydney. The senior lecturers were trying to get into our pants.'

'How about the professors?'

'They were already in—some of them, and some pants.'

The waiter hovered with the menus.

'I want fish, salad and white wine,' she said. 'How about you?'

'Steak, potatoes and red wine.'

The waiter beamed. 'So refreshing, the difference,' he said. 'Leave it to me. I'll bring you both the very best.'

We handed him the menus. Oddly, after the initial rapport, we were both silent for a minute as the restaurant noise buzzed around us and the sounds of the Quay carried faintly through.

The wine arrived—her riesling in an ice bucket, my merlot naked. Our waiter poured and we both waived the tasting ritual. He stood aside to let another waiter put small plates in front of us, fried whitebait for her, grilled mushrooms for me.

'Enterprising chap,' I said. 'Do they know you here?'

She smiled and didn't answer. We drank some wine and started in on the food.

'Tell me something interesting you did today,' I said.

She told me about researching a cache of military weapons found on a building site at Coogee. World War I stuff. 'Well before your time, but I thought you'd be interested, having been in the army.'

'How did you know that?'

'You're in the records, Cliff. No getting away from it.'

The mains arrived.

'Now you,' she said.

I spoke about a man coming back from exile. A man with a secret and a score to settle as well as a Damoclean sword hanging over his head.

'It's much the same line of work, isn't it? The past impacting on the present.'

I savoured a mouthful of excellent eye fillet. 'It's central to you, I guess. For me it often explains things, but I have to deal in the here and now.'

We caught the ferry to Balmain and stood outside sheltered from the breeze and holding each other.

'How long since you did this?'

'Alone or with a beautiful woman?'

She dug me in the ribs. 'None of your blarney. How Irish are you?'

'About half. How about you?'

'Much the same. Troy must have been an assumed name picked up somewhere.'

'I like it.'

'Could be worse. Could've been Athens.'

I laughed. 'To answer your question, I can't remember the last ferry ride but I think the last time I was afloat here my assistant and I rowed out to a boat and found a dead man. This is a whole lot better.'

'That's to remind me that you're a tough guy?'

I kissed her. 'No, at a time like this it's to remind myself.'

We did the long walk to her place, sticking close together and not saying much. We went in and, still with a minimum of speech, we undressed each other and made love with a dimmed-down light on.

She fell asleep almost at once and I propped up on one elbow and looked at her. The signs of strain that I'd seen on her face at our earlier meetings were smoothed away by sleep. I imagined a police artist being asked to draw her from my description: translucent skin, strong nose and jaw, heavy brow. Feature by feature it'd take a good artist to capture her beauty, which was a matter of how the features blended together.

I fell asleep and dreamed a mélange of Hawes, Cathy Carter, Frank Parker and Paul the bikie all doing an incomprehensible mixture of things they'd never do.

*

Over a very early breakfast, Alicia in a flowered silk kimono and me in my shirt with a towel around my waist, my mobile bleeped with an email from Nils Olquist.

Alicia lifted an eyebrow the way some people can and others never master. 'Important?'

'Yes.'

'I'll get dressed.'

I punched in the password, my fingers clumsy on the small keys. The message said that Henderson was financially embarrassed and contained an address in Haberfield and numbers for a landline and a mobile phone.

Alicia came out in a pants suit again, this time beige, with a red shirt. She was transferring things from a bag that had matched her outfit of yesterday to today's version.

'Fiddly stuff you blokes don't have to bother about,' she said. 'But then again, I don't need to shave. I have to go, Cliff. Just close the door hard and I'll leave it to you to contact me next time. Okay?'

'I will.' I stood and the towel fell off.

She looked me up and down. 'I hope so, I really do.'

A quick kiss and she was gone.

I dressed, called a cab and had the driver use his GPS to locate the address. It turned out to be opposite a stretch of Haberfield parkland bisected by a canal. The driver slowed and I told him to keep going and then turn back, stop and wait. He looked puzzled and did it. The house was a large California bungalow set on a big block with a chest-high wall in the front.

I rang the mobile number Nils had given me and hung up as soon as a male voice answered. After a few minutes a man in pyjamas and dressing gown came through the gate in the wall and looked at his doorstep, squinted at the path, then scrabbled in the shrubbery and retrieved a rolled-up newspaper before going back inside.

About twenty minutes later the gate in the wall opened again and he stepped out, this time with an Old English sheepdog on a leash. The cab's clock showed precisely 8 am. The dog walker was in his sixties, heavily built and more rugged-up against the cool morning air than seemed necessary. He crossed the road and took a path that wound through the park.

'Where to now, sir?' the Asian taxi driver said, sounding troubled.

I had no idea how long the dog walk would take but it wouldn't be long enough to organise a reception committee— meaning me, Soames and Paul's soldiers—to intercept him. And I couldn't be entirely sure the man was Henderson. Could've been a visitor or a professional dog walker. I told the driver there was nothing to worry about and asked him to take me to Glebe. I gave him a big tip with Timothy Greenhall's money.

At home, I phoned Soames. 'Describe Henderson to me.'

'Jesus, it's been years. No idea what he looks like now.'

'Height? Weight?'

'Medium, getting fat when I last saw him.'

'Anything distinctive?'

A pause. 'He was a cold-blooded bastard. I don't mean in the character sense. He felt the cold. He was always wearing extra layers.'

'Tell me he was a dog lover.'

'He was. He bred Old English sheepdogs. Dopey animals, in my book, but he was nutty about them.'

I told him that I'd spotted Henderson and that he'd begun his walk at a precise time, on the hour. Probably his usual routine. Soames said that was Henderson to a tee. A stickler for time.

'I'll ring Paul,' I said, 'and set up an intercept for tomorrow morning. It's an ideal spot. Leave it for a bit and then you liaise with him. Can you be convincing about having the torch?'

'I don't have to be. Chas knows I have it. And I can be convincing about using it. Don't worry.'

I rang Paul and told him what I'd told Soames.

'You want me there with the brothers, at the east end of the park?'

'That's right. Bring ten bad ones.'

'You haven't said which house. You don't trust us.'

'Right again.'

'I'll keep that in mind, and, Hardy, there better not be anyone else there except Luke. Understand?'

'Yes. Have you got anyone who's good with dogs?'

'Yes.'

'Bring him and supply him with whatever sheepdogs like to eat at eight o'clock in the morning.'

That got me the last word with him for the first time.

25

With a day to fill in, I drove to Erskineville and paid Nils his five thousand. He took it with a becoming reluctance. It was a little too early for the aquavit, even for Nils, so we drank coffee. He started to explain the difficulties he'd experienced but I stopped him.

'I wouldn't understand a tenth of it, mate. Just tell me you got in and out without leaving a trace.'

'I did, yes.'

'A hundred per cent?'

'Ninety-nine point nine. Only a fool claims a hundred per cent success at anything.'

'That's true.'

'Cliff, I'm a little worried. I've noticed a bikie hanging around over the last couple of days. Maybe not the same one, even. I'm wondering if Trudie . . .'

'Nils, I can set your mind at rest. Nothing to do with Trudie, everything to do with what you've just done for me.

I guarantee you won't see a bikie again unless you go looking for one.'

Nils looked relieved at first and then concerned. 'Bikies, police . . . I hope you know what you're doing.'

'I hope so, too,' I said.

I went to the gym and spent longer there than usual having a thorough workout and then a sauna and a spa. Wesley Scott gave me an ironic look as I left.

'Going to war, Cliff?'

'Just a skirmish.'

'How many of your nine lives you got left, man?'

'Just enough, Wes,' I said. 'Just enough.'

My mobile rang as I was getting into my car.

'Cliff, this is Cathy Carter.'

'Cathy.'

'I'm sorry I . . . went to water. I want to know what's going on. Can we meet?'

There was something I urgently needed to know about the Hawes voice record and she was the only one likely to be able to tell me. We arranged to meet at three-thirty in a coffee bar in the complex in Liverpool Road that housed the Ashfield Council Chambers, the library and other enterprises. The arrangement left me time for a drink, just one, and a focaccia at the Bar Napoli.

Cathy Carter, when I finally located her in one of the several coffee bars, was looking a whole lot better with her hair freshly washed and shining and wearing jeans and an oversize sweater. She gave me a smile as we shook hands.

'You seem tired,' she said.

'Thanks, I'm working on a look that'll show clients how hard I'm working.'

'Always joking. I'm sorry about destroying Colin's disks. It was a stupid thing to do. A waste of what he wanted and . . . Are you still going after them?'

'Yes, and getting closer.'

'Is there any way I can help? I've been racking my brains, but I was never on the inside with what was happening.'

'There is one thing . . .'

'I've become a coffee addict,' she said. 'What will you have?'

'A very hot flat white.'

She jumped up and went to the counter. The physical sprightliness was part of her determined effort to bounce back. I admired her and had an impulse to tell her what was happening. I repressed it because the outcome was as uncertain as a politician's promise. She came back and sat, straight-backed and gallant.

'You were saying?'

I decided she deserved some information. 'One thing worried me about the snippet I heard from Colin's disk. We're actually targeting . . .'

'We?'

'I've got help from some unlikely quarters.'

She nodded. The coffee arrived and we did things with the spoons, the way you do.

'We're targeting a man named Charles Henderson, also known as Chas.'

'He was mentioned on the disk.'

'Right. It's possible that the other person he was talking to is the real villain of the piece. You didn't recognise the voices?'

'No. I assume Colin burned the disk from the surveillance phone-taps. I never knew who the task force was targeting.'

'Well, it was a long shot. Why d'you think Colin copied them and brought them home?'

'He didn't trust everybody. He was sure there were leaks. I suppose he was going to play you the disks to convince you he was on the same side, to get you to help him find out what was going on. If any current police were involved.'

It made sense.

She told me that her application for stress leave had been approved.

'So you're going to stay in the force?'

'I'm going to the top,' she said.

'Good for you, and know what? I think I can help you.'

I picked up a Bravado escort somewhere between Ashfield and Pyrmont. I didn't know whether to be comforted or threatened. It was clear that Paul had at least some of the gang under his control, but for how long? And what kind of exploit would it take for him to confirm that control? The last thing I wanted was a bikie killing, either at Haberfield or Camden. I completed the drive in a state of apprehension. The bikie peeled off a block away from my office, but there are half a dozen different places from which to watch a building that has no back exit. Even if it did, Paul would have the manpower to watch the two exits and the car.

Things didn't improve when Frank Parker rang.

'Haven't heard from you in a while, Cliff. What's happening?'

It was one of the times I couldn't be open with Frank. What Soames, Paul and I were planning was full of dangerous possibilities and highly illegal to begin with. I couldn't draw Frank into the scheme, he had too much to lose.

'Still working,' I said.

'Cliff, I'm hearing disconcerting whispers.'

'About what, Frank?'

'About you and the company you're keeping. And a ... what looks like a defensive attitude.'

So my bikie escort had been reported on and my presence at the Colin Hawes wake. 'Are you giving me a warning, Frank?'

'I wouldn't put it quite like that. I just hope you're not off on some cowboy pursuit that could lead you into serious trouble.'

'Trouble is my business.'

'This is no joke. Information came through to us that you were at the scene of the Dusty Miller killing.'

'Yeah, I beat him to death with a weighted torch after torturing him for an hour or two until he told me where his gun stash was and now I'm hoping to reduce my mortgage with the proceeds of its sale. Who's this we, Frank?'

'The group I told you about, trying to unscramble the GCU mess.'

'Past and present?'

'As much as possible.'

'That's not good enough. Your group's likely to come up with names that have to be protected for the sake of the force. It might even find people who're protecting the ones still killing and making dirty money. There's been too much covering up, Frank, and you know it. It's time for the light of day to shine on the past and present.'

'You've located Rooster Fowler, right?'

'No comment.'

'Cliff, Cliff, there're eyes open everywhere. Someone from Soames-Wetherell's office reported on a meeting you had there. I'm betting Luke Soames was there, and I'd trust him as far as I would Alan Jones.'

I realised then that Frank had been probing for a purpose, working to an agenda that I had to hope was not entirely his own.

'Come out with it, Frank. What's this call all about?'

There was a long pause. 'I'm sticking my neck out making

the call at all. Fact is there's a feeling that you should either be held and questioned . . .'

'What for?'

'That's the softer line—for failing to report Miller's murder. The harder line is to put you out of circulation permanently by stripping you of your licence and prosecuting you for conspiracy.'

'When, either way?'

'Soon.'

'Thanks, Frank. I appreciate it. I just wish you'd told me upfront before you started trying to pull my strings.'

His voice was a whisper. 'Yes, me too.'

26

We were all in position the following day, ten minutes before 8 am. Soames was looking distinguished in a suit and light overcoat; Paul and his ten bikies had gone to town on their hair, beards and uniforms. There's something distinctly threatening about a denim jacket from which the arms have been ripped out or cut off with blunt scissors leaving ragged edges. Although the morning was almost cold, several of the bikies were bare-armed with tatts showing. One had a tattooed face, dreads and looked like an uglier version of Mel Gibson in *Braveheart*.

Right on time Henderson appeared with the sheepdog. He wore a heavy coat and a scarf and seemed more stooped than the morning before, but that might just have been because I was beginning to feel sorry for him. The dog pulled at the leash and wanted to cross the road even though a car was coming, and Henderson had trouble holding it back. A dopey breed of dog, as Soames had said.

Paul slipped automatically into the CO role. 'Does he cross that bridge, Hardy?'

'Headed that way yesterday.'

'Creature of habit,' Paul said, turning to his troops. 'Half of you head back that way and cross the canal and the rest come up as soon as he steps on the bridge. Hem the fucker in. Medium revs, but keep 'em revving.'

'Do we go onto the fuckin' bridge?' the tattoo-faced bikie asked.

'Do whatever you think is scariest but, Kurt, make sure he can see you.'

'He's getting there,' I said.

Paul started his engine. 'Go!'

The bikes roared off in two directions and Soames and I walked slowly towards the bridge.

'What d'you think of our Paulie?' Soames asked.

'He impresses me and worries me.'

'Always did. Can you imagine how his mum felt about him?'

'No. What about his dad?'

'Mercenary, killed in Angola in the late eighties.'

Under the direction of the mercenary's son, the trap was sprung perfectly. By the time we got there, Henderson was in the middle of the bridge with the two bikie teams at either end, their engines rumbling. Kurt had run his bike up close to Henderson and a member of Paul's team who'd ridden pillion had advanced from the near side, cut the leash and was feeding tidbits to the acquiescent dog. As we approached, Paul slammed his gloves together with a crack that sounded above the engines. He made a cutting gesture and the bikes sputtered and fell silent.

Soames stepped onto the bridge. 'Hello, Chas,' he said. 'How's it going?'

Henderson had been transfixed by the ugliness of Kurt. Now he stared at Soames through thick-lensed glasses. 'Do I know you?'

'Luke Soames.'

Henderson gripped the bridge's rail to steady himself. 'Jesus Christ.'

'Yeah, risen from the dead,' Soames said. 'You're going to help me put Rooster Fowler out of business.'

'No,' Henderson said.

'Yes, or the boys here are set to put you in the canal—a bit here and a bit there and a bit further off.'

Henderson's puffy red face paled. He stared at the bikies as if just beginning to appreciate how they connected with him and Fowler. As he made the connection, Kurt's smile, splitting the bizarrely marked face, was horrible.

'I didn't kill Miller,' Henderson spluttered.

'We know that,' Paul said. 'You wouldn't have the balls. But you know who did and we're going to make him pay—with your help.'

'I've still got the torch, Chas,' Soames said. 'With blood and the prints and the DNA, and I'll use it.'

Traffic was building and other dog walkers and a few joggers were coming into the park. They'd avoid the bikie pack for a while but some would get on their mobiles.

'We'll have to adjourn this,' I said.

Soames nodded. 'Who's at home, Chas?'

Henderson looked relieved at the mere mention of the word. 'No one. Betty died two years ago and the kids are scattered.'

'Let's go,' Paul said. 'Stu, mind the dog.' He gave a thumbs-up to the other bikies. 'Thanks, guys. See you at the hill later.'

The engines started. Kurt gave Henderson a last leer and wheeled his bike back off the bridge. Soames, Henderson and I started down the path back to the road. Paul rode ahead of us and parked immediately outside Henderson's house. Trust him to have taken note of which one it was.

Henderson was quiet, probably wondering how he could get out of the fix he was in. Soames gave him no room for doubt.

'If you don't do what we say, Chas, the next time you step outside that gate you're a dead man.'

'I've got friends,' Henderson said.

'You're broke,' I said. 'And broke ex-cops haven't got any friends, not really.'

'Who the fuck are you?'

'My name's Hardy. I'm working for someone you probably still think of as Tommy Greenfall.'

Henderson stopped in his tracks. 'Working how?'

'I'm a private detective investigating the murder of his son.'

Henderson looked at me through his pebble glasses. 'We might be able to work something out.'

Stu was ahead of us, playing with the dog, running away and letting the dog catch him for a reward. Henderson looked at the play bleakly as if he'd lost his only friend. Maybe he had.

Soames prodded him back into focus. 'Don't be too sure about that. It's a side issue. We've got Rooster dead to rights, as they say in those English cop shows, for killing Roy Carlton. You were there.'

'Not really,' Henderson said.

Soames was a master at this. 'Well, that could be negotiable.'

Paul, back with us, contained his impatience with difficulty as we waited to cross the road. Once across, he held out his hand to Henderson. 'Keys,' he said.

It was an old technique but a good one—strip the person you're targeting of every bit of control. Stu was standing by, petting the dog. Henderson handed over the keys. Paul unlocked the gate and we entered a garden so neglected it shocked even me, a non-gardener. The grass was knee-high; the shrubs had grown out of control and the trees had dropped leaves and some branches. There was a rank smell of decayed vegetable matter, and weeds had almost taken over the gravel path to the porch.

'Jesus, Chas,' Soames said. 'You've let things slip.'

Paul had gone ahead, mounted the steps to the porch, kicked aside a tattered doormat and opened the door.

Soames shook his head in disgust. 'Hope it's not as bad inside.'

'It's worse,' Henderson said.

He was right—the house smelled and looked uncared-for from the front passage through to the back sunroom. Dust had trapped the stink of cigarette smoke, takeaway food, unwashed clothes, rising damp, mould and dog. The long back yard was a jungle with wisteria threatening to envelop an aluminium shed and the Hills hoist.

The living-room furniture consisted of a once presentable couch and chair set now scratched and torn and covered with dog hair. Soames sneezed violently as soon as he entered. Henderson suddenly seemed uplifted by the squalor.

'Allergic to dogs, are you, Luke?'

'I'm allergic to filth.'

Paul pushed Henderson down into a chair and stood over him.

'You shut up and listen.'

Soames brushed the dog hair and ash from the arm of a chair and sat. 'You're going to ring Rooster Fowler, tell him I'm going to give the cops the evidence he knows I've got and you're going to testify against him.'

Henderson shook his head. 'No way, and I can't ring him. I don't even know where he is.'

'Hardy?' Paul said.

I took a punt. 'We know you've been in touch with him. We have a record of a conversation where you discuss the security of the line, among other more serious things.'

Henderson peeled off his scarf but left his heavy coat on. 'Bit vague, that. Recorded by whom?'

'By the late Acting Sergeant Colin Hawes of the GCU, that's *whom*. Also beaten to death by your old mate.'

Henderson's myopic eyes flicked over the three of us. 'He's no mate of mine and I can't contact him. He contacts me.'

'I know where he is,' I said. 'You can have a chat.'

'He'll kill me.'

'No he won't,' Paul said. 'I guarantee it. And your protection. But I'll kill you if you don't cooperate. I guarantee that as well.'

Henderson pulled a pack of cigarettes from his coat pocket, fumbled one up to his mouth and lit it shakily. He inhaled deeply.

'Fowler won't believe you'll use the torch. It's your insurance.'

'I've got cancer, Chas,' Soames said. 'I'm a ticking time bomb. I don't need insurance. Funeral insurance maybe.'

Henderson puffed away, flicking ash on himself and the carpet. He looked at Paul. 'Protection?'

Paul nodded. 'During the trial and after.'

'I get immunity?' Henderson said to no one in particular.

I said, 'Fowler could be cited for three or more murders. You give evidence on a few of them, I'd say you'd be granted immunity because the prosecution'll need everything it can get.'

'Christ,' Henderson said, 'it'll almost be a relief. That fucker . . .'

'Save it,' Paul said. 'We're at the crunch, Hardy. I hope you've got a plan.'

'I have. The first thing is to keep Chas here under wraps.'

'I've got a nice suite at the Connaught,' Soames said. 'He could be my guest for a few days.'

'You're not cutting us out are you, Hardy?' Paul said.

'No. You're essential. It'll take a day or so to set up. How would your blokes like a ride down to Camden?'

'They'd love it.'

'I'm pretty sure that's where Fowler is. They'll be needed to do something similar to what they did today.'

Paul nodded.

Soames sneezed again and this time he fought for breath. 'I have to get out of here,' he wheezed.

'Well let's go to the Connaught,' I said. 'A few tasty things must've been plotted there. Wasn't Mr Rent-a-Kill a resident once? What was his name again?'

Soames was standing with a handkerchief up to his face. 'Chris Flannery. When I was undercover I once watched him strangle someone.'

Paul, who'd made being unimpressed an artform, reacted. 'Shit. Who?'

'Someone who thoroughly deserved it,' Soames said.

Henderson heaved himself out of the chair. Going to the Connaught apparently appealed to him. Then he heard barking from outside and turned anxiously to Paul.

'What about my dog?'

Paul grinned. 'Call it a hostage. Stu'll take care of it. What's its name?'

Henderson had smoked his cigarette down to the filter and snuffed it out with his stained fingers. He flicked it away and picked up his scarf. 'Roger.'

'That's appropriate,' Soames said.

27

After Henderson had packed a bag and farewelled the dog, Soames drove him to the Connaught in his rented Saab. I dawdled along behind, turning over my plan in my mind and considering the only alternative—to lay out the whole thing for Frank Parker. Reluctantly, I had to reject that: I had no idea who the members of his group were and I had no confidence that there wouldn't be a leak to Fowler. I didn't know the extent of Rooster's network still intact inside the police but I couldn't take a chance. I knew I was putting my relationship with Frank on the block again, but my confidence now lay with Paul, Soames and Cathy Carter. They were the cards I'd drawn and I was determined to play them.

Soames's suite was not far short of palatial, with double glazing protection against the traffic three floors below and a view out over Hyde Park with the spiritual uplift coming from trees or church steeples, depending on your preference.

Soames settled Henderson into the second bedroom and told him to stay there. Soames and I sat at a table in the broad, well-lit, temperature-controlled living space with a bottle of Johnnie Walker Black and a bowl of ice.

'Not too early for you, Hardy? I hear you're a gymaholic.'

'It's afternoon in Auckland,' I said.

Soames poured.

'Ever been a smoker, Hardy?' he asked, shifting my glass across to me.

'A long time ago.'

'Find it hard to quit?'

'No.'

'Next question for you . . . Cliff. How much have you told Frank Parker?'

Intelligence, or cunning, or both, seemed to be in the Soames/Wetherell genes. I'd been in enough military and legal conferences to know that there's usually a critical question to be answered before the group can get down to business. The sharpest mind asked it and here it was.

'Nothing,' I said.

'Why not? He's been your friend and saviour for years. At times you could hardly have operated without him.'

'That's true,' I said, 'and I'm not going into any details. Frank knows I'm working for Timothy Greenhall and that I have suspicions about Fowler. He doesn't know that I've found Fowler or that I have . . . allies. Not really.'

'What does that mean?'

'He knows something about the bikies, but he knows absolutely nothing about the ... methodology I have in mind for snaring Fowler.'

'You're putting a long-term close relationship at risk.'

'I know, and I'm pissed off about it, but that's the way it is.'

Soames leaned back and drank some whisky. I did the same.

'It's time I heard something about that methodology,' Soames said.

That night Paul and I took a trip out to Camden to look Fowler's place over. It was dark when we arrived but the driveway from the gate to the main buildings was well lit and there seemed to be lights around the buildings themselves.

'Heavy carbon footprint,' I said.

'I wonder the horses can sleep.'

I tried to remember the layout on the website. 'I think the horses are down the back somewhere.'

Then more lights flicked off and, after a pause, on again.

'Sensors,' Paul said. 'There's people moving about.'

'Be good to know how many and what kind. We have to get closer.'

'Wouldn't the fence have an alarm?'

'Long fence. Let's try up there where it goes closer to the house.'

We worked our way along the fence line, keeping to the

scrub a metre or two back from it. We reached a point where we'd be able to see more of what went on near the house through Paul's night-vision goggles. The fence was a chest-high mesh affair and if it was electrified there was no sign of it. Paul slung the glasses around his neck, put his hands on the top of the fence and prepared to jump. Yet another light went on near a building close to the house and several dogs began to bark.

'Shit.' Paul moved back and we scrambled deeper into the scrub. Two men and two dogs arrived at the spot within a minute and we could see them clearly enough in the light of their torches. Big men, both with handguns.

'Could be a fuckin' wallaby,' one of the men said. 'It's happened before.'

'Call the boss.'

'He's probably in the sack with Queenie.'

'Shut your face. Call him.'

A mobile phone lit up.

'It's me. We thought we heard something outside, but there's nothing we can see . . . Right. Understood.'

'What does he say?'

'He says stay alert and let two more dogs loose.'

They retreated with the still growling dogs and Paul and I waited until it was safe to move.

'*Formidable*,' Paul said.

'Right. It's a flush-out job.'

*

It took a while to organise, but by early evening the following day Soames, Henderson, Cathy Carter and I were in a motel close to the Top Gun Bloodstock property. About thirty Bravados were posted around the perimeter of the place with a concentration near the only drivable exit. A couple of the bikies were armed with shotguns. A set of spikes embedded in a heavy rubber strip was stretched across the road just outside the Top Gun gate. All we had were a couple of mobile phones and a computer.

'You're sure they'll have Skype?' Cathy said. She was in uniform, looking nervous.

'I'm told they all do,' I said. 'They need to talk to owners and breeders face to face, as it were.'

'You're well enough rehearsed, Chas,' Soames said. 'Make the call.'

Henderson had trouble with the buttons so I dialled the number for him.

'Top Gun.'

'This is Charlie Henderson. Listen very carefully. Tell Rooster to log on to Skype. This is my Skype name— RoyCarlton, one word. He'll understand.'

'Just a minute.' He ended the call.

'Pretty good, Chas,' Soames said.

Henderson was sweating inside his heavy clothes. 'Can I have a smoke, for Christ's sake?'

'When it's over,' Soames said.

Our computer was booted up and ready to go. We stared at the screen, willing it to come to life. It flickered and then a man appeared sitting full square in front of us. He was big, broad-shouldered, with strong, regular features. His eyebrows were dark and his thick, wavy hair was grey. He wore a checked shirt and a knitted tie. His right hand went up to his ear and he fiddled with a hearing aid.

'What's this, Chas?'

We'd put Henderson in plain view. Now he slid to one side and Soames appeared on the screen next to him. I'd briefed Soames about the voice recording.

'Gidday, Rooster,' Soames said.

To give him his due, Fowler barely reacted. 'Luke, you queer cunt. This is just like old times.'

'No it's not, Rooster. This is the end of old times forever.'

'You look a bit sick, Luke. Thin, like.'

'I am. That's why I don't care what happens to me from here on . . .'

'What about your little petunias in lotus land?'

'They'll be all right.'

'What's Chas up to?'

'He's going to testify about you killing Roy Carlton and the Greenhall kid.'

Fowler was gesturing, issuing unspoken instructions to people offscreen. 'No evidence there, mate.'

'There's a voice recording of you and Chas chatting.'

'Yeah? Made by who?'

'They tell me his name was Colin Hawes and there're questions to be asked about his death as well. You're ratshit, Rooster, to use your own expression.'

Fowler's eyes went narrow. 'Why're you doing this, Luke? You got in for your share back then.'

'Let's say I want a clear conscience for my exit.'

'Bullshit.'

'And I have a nephew who's big in the Bravados and wants to have a few quiet words with you about Dusty Miller. Maybe not all that quiet.'

The screen went blank.

'He's up and running,' I said. 'Let's move.'

We arrived at the property in time to see one of the Bravados use bolt cutters on the padlock and three loud-revving bikes roar up the drive and circle the house with headlights blazing and motors screaming. Dogs barked and I heard shots.

'I hope they're not shooting the dogs,' I said.

Paul was astride his bike, dying to get into the action but, like a true general, knowing where his place was. 'Not with Kurt in charge,' he said. 'That's Fowler's men shooting at moving targets.'

The bikes returned and twenty headlights were trained on the drive as two cars appeared from beside the house. Big Mercs, their headlights on full beam, they roared towards us, went through the gate and the first car ran into the spiked mat the Bravados had lined across the road. It slewed wildly and the second car was forced to slow. Two bikies blew out the front tyres of both cars and the second crashed into the first. A man jumped out of each car with a handgun raised to look into the barrels of sawn-off shotguns held by men with balaclavas and attitude.

'Be brave, arsehole,' one of the bikies who'd seen too many Dirty Harry movies said, and both men dropped their guns.

The whole area was lit up by headlights with the smell of burning rubber and gunsmoke in the air. I approached the first car and saw a big, grey-haired man in the back holding a small, sobbing woman in his arms, their faces washed white by the lights.

Some of the bikies had been drinking, or taking drugs, and they were hot for more action. Paul was having trouble controlling them when he made the call to us.

Cathy strode forward. Thinner than before, standing very straight with her cap and her buttons glinting, she looked commanding. With me beside her she marched up to the first car and gestured for the back door to be opened. It was and Fowler and the woman, her heavy makeup smudged by tears, stared up at her.

'Grantley Fowler,' Cathy said, 'I am arresting you in connection with the deaths of Roy Carlton, Patrick Greenhall, Herbert Miller and . . . Acting Police Sergeant Colin Hawes. You don't have to say anything, but anything you do say will be recorded and may be used in evidence against you.'

28

It was a long drawn-out story after that, with legal difficulties of all sorts to untangle. Fowler's high-powered and expensive legal team tried to argue that the arrest was unorthodox to the point of illegality, which it was. But guns, a specially weighted torch, a large quantity of drugs, false passports and cash found in Fowler's car overcame that objection.

Cathy explained how she'd enlisted the help of the bikies and how I'd worked to facilitate the evidence from Soames and Henderson. Several of Fowler's minions put pressure on by agreeing to cooperate with the prosecution. At times it was touch and go, but eventually Soames's evidence (he'd kept the torch in a climate-controlled wine storage locker) and Henderson's testimony proved decisive.

Fowler was convicted of the murder of police informer Roy Carlton and sentenced to twenty years' gaol. A government-backed suit claiming that his assets were the proceeds of crime was successful and property and funds were seized. The ex-model he'd married, and who'd posed and cavorted in different fetching outfits throughout the trial, divorced him.

Although no charge was brought against Fowler for the killing of Patrick Greenhall, Herbert Miller or Colin Hawes, Timothy Greenhall and Cathy Carter had to be satisfied with the outcome.

Greenhall secured his investment and announced that he was devoting a substantial part of the profits he derived to establishing scholarships for medical research. I had a final meeting with him. The knowledge that his shady past had brought about the death of his son had had an effect on him. He looked older and was less assertive. He paid me a healthy bonus. That proved useful, as I took a long furlough.

A few details of Greenhall's involvement with Fowler emerged at the trial and he stepped down from the chairmanship of Precision Instruments. The company still holds a strong position on the stock market and Harry Tickener tells me the word is that Greenhall is still in control by proxy.

Paul Soames, or Wetherell, or whatever, dropped out of sight. Luke Soames returned to Thailand and, granted immunity for his testimony against Fowler, Henderson moved to Queensland, where I suppose he found people to talk to about the good old days. Bit hot up there for Roger, though.

My strained relationship with Frank Parker remained that way, a casualty of the case. He was hurt that I hadn't confided in him and maintained his 'committee' would never have leaked. That was the word he used and it confirmed my doubts—I had an inbuilt, possibly irrational, distrust of committees.

With Rooster and Henderson out of the game, the task force was able to proceed more openly, and speedily—those senior police and politicians who'd covered for them now lying very low. At least Frank was pleased about that.

I spent much of my long break with Alicia Troy. She'd secured a grant to research the relics of whaling operations around Australia. We travelled by 4WD, light plane and boat to well-known and little-known coastal places—harbours, ports and estuaries subject to constant change by winds, tides and shifting sands.

After the trip we both went back to work with renewed energy and gradually, for both of us, our affair became a memory anchored nostalgically in time and a hundred places.

The silence from Paul, who'd played such a crucial part in the case, troubled me and I rang Soames-Wetherell to ask about him. Before answering, the lawyer told me he was in the process of arranging visas for Luke Soames's family, consisting of his male lover and the lover's two children.

'Tricky business,' he said. 'Particularly with our new masters at the helm.'

'I can imagine. What about Paul?'

'Taken with him, weren't you?'

'I could never make up my mind about him.'

'No one can. I have heard from him recently. He's concerned about the moves to declare the motorcycle clubs illegal organisations and wondering if some kind of incorporation device might be a counter to that.'

'Could it?'

'It's an interesting question.'

A month later I got a phone call at 6 am.

'Hardy, this is Paul Soames. You'll be interested in an item on the front page of today's paper.'

'Have to wait. I don't get the paper delivered any more. I got tired of it being nicked or getting the wrong one.'

'You've got one this morning. Take a look.'

The paper was on the doorstep. The headline read: FORMER COP KILLED IN PRISON and the article went on:

Former New South Wales Detective Inspector Grantley 'Rooster' Fowler, who was serving twenty years for murder, was stabbed to death in Bathurst prison yesterday. Bill 'Loopy' Deling, a former member of the Bravados motorcycle gang, also serving a life sentence, admitted to the killing, saying it was in revenge for Fowler's murder of Herbert 'Dusty' Miller, Bravados boss, in Katoomba last year. Officials said Deling had taken advantage of a temporary relaxation of Fowler's status as a protected prisoner while he was being treated for illnesses connected with his alcoholism.

I fully expect to hear about Paul Soames again, although in what connection—political, legal, financial—is anybody's guess.